To A.

# LOUIS

### SUPERNATURAL PRISON BOOK 6

### JAYMIN EVE

**Jaymin Eve**
**Louis: Supernatural Prison #6**

Editing: Lee from Oceans Edge Editing and Liv from Hot Tree Editing
Cover: Tamara Kokic

*For Teresa.*
*You claimed Louis as a mate, and I think you might love him*
*almost as much as I do.*
*Thank you for being a wonderful friend.*

# 1

## LOUIS

*D*eath. Pain. Burning.

Coherent thought was less frequent now as I slowly lost my battle with the darkness. Darkness was part of every magic user, usually suppressed by the light inside of us, but now ... now my strength to keep it contained was fading. I couldn't even get any messages through to my brother, Quale, anymore, and my family ... I could no longer see them.

Jessa and the Compasses.

I'd almost died trying to save them.

*My true family.*

I was the weakest I'd ever been, which gave the demons the opening they had been waiting for. The soul chains clanked as I yanked against them, flickers of fury burning inside of my chest—or the place my chest would be if I was still in my physical body. Right now I existed as nothing more than a soul, which, truth be told, was the most important part of any being. It was the eternal part, and the demons knew this was where the true power lay.

Fire slashed across my essence again and again. I'd experienced a full range of pain over the years, from agonizing physical torture to an emotional loss that had come very close to completely crushing my soul. I thought there was nothing that could hurt more than losing my chosen mate and her family—who had become my family as well—but these demons were very ... inventive.

The circus of souls, where I had spent an unknown amount of time, was filled with stolen essences. The demons used the magic that was held in our souls to power their world—the land between—a purgatory with no natural energy. The ley lines of this world were dead, but they had found a very inventive way to keep themselves functioning.

It was here that the trapped demons schemed and plotted to try and gain access to Faerie or Earth, where a plethora of energy and souls waited for them. I would do anything to stop them from leaving this land, even sacrifice myself. Blocking demons from leaving the land between was something I'd been working toward for many years, from the time of the jeweled princesses.

My family continued this fight. I'd felt the Lebron-Compass energy at the portal. We'd all just managed to keep the demons from being released.

*Family.*

Somehow they'd wormed their way into my heart—despite my best efforts to prevent close connections. I'd finally found my family, and the knowledge that I might not be around much longer to enjoy them caused true sorrow within me. Even if I didn't die, the darkness inside my magic, the darkness all sorcerers held, was growing in power. My light was fading, and if that happened I would lose myself.

Darkness would rule me.

## ELIZABETH TERESA MONTGOMERY II

*T*he medical file at the end of his bed taunted me. Louis had been a pain in my ass for more years than I could remember. We grew up together and had been the best of friends. Then he had fallen in love with my sister, and ... everything changed. But he had seen me—and my family—at our best and worst, and I thought I had seen him at his, but *this*, his body so still ... lifeless ... it was heartbreaking. Far worse than I could have ever imagined.

I'd spent over half my life missing and hating him in equal measure, and it still bothered me to see him like this. It bothered me a lot.

Moving closer to his side, I reached out and pushed a strand of his light hair back. "Louis, come on, I need you to wake up so I can get out of here. I need to crawl back into my little hole. There's too much world out here for me." I'd even take a moment of having to stare into those arresting purple eyes that saw far too much, just to see he was okay.

"Lizzie."

The feminine voice said my name with a bite of command. I had never been very good at taking orders, even if they were unstated, so I took my time turning. Standing in the doorway was a very young, very beautiful wolf shifter.

Jessa Lebron, the chosen dragon marked who had helped to defeat Larkspur. A pang of guilt hit me then—I'd been avoiding her as much as possible. Louis had called for me during their battle against the dragon king and I had ignored him. I had let them all down. I should have been here for that fight. But I just ... couldn't. I could not be in one more war. I'd already lost everything, every single being I cared about. I was done.

And if I was really honest, seeing Louis again might have actually broken me.

I raised an eyebrow as she stared at me. "Yes?" I finally said.

She shook her head. "Oh, sorry, I'm staring. It's just that you're kinda a big deal." She winked then, and I couldn't help but laugh. Jessa was charming, there was no denying it. Her blue eyes twinkled as she took a few steps closer. "The real reason I'm here is that we have some news about Louis. We got back yesterday from Faerie, and Grace is a princess, and so much shit happened. But the important thing is that we learned Louis is stuck in the land of the demons. His brother has been able to communicate with him ... kind of, anyway. His soul was captured and dragged there in the last battle with Kristoff. We need to go and rescue him."

"Fuck..." The light bulb above our heads shattered. It took me a few moments to realize it was *my* loss of control which caused the explosion. Holy hell, I hadn't lost hold of my energy for years. Decades, even. Jessa never even flinched. Clearly, volatile magic did not bother her.

"You swear?" she said with a grin. "I never expected that from you, I guess because you're so ... pretty."

Despite my current disbelief, I couldn't help but smile. "Firstly, you're pretty, and I'm guessing you enjoy a curse word or two." She shrugged and nodded, not even attempting to deny it. "And secondly, I was the bad girl of my time. 'Ladies don't curse' was the most used phrase around me."

Before she could comment on that, and she was definitely amused, I turned the conversation back to the important facts. "The land of demons? His soul has been there this entire time?"

No wonder there had been nothing I could do to bring him back. He was trapped with beings far worse than anything Earth knew. Louis was the last of my family, even though we hadn't treated each other as such for many years. Not since we lost Regina.

*Lost.* Such an insignificant word for her *murder*. Stolen. Torn. Destroyed. Much closer, but still not enough.

"We're going to get him back," Jessa continued, ripping me from the pain of old memories. "The Compasses are just sorting out bullshit council details, gathering supplies, and then we're heading back to Faerie. Pretty much straight away."

I nodded. "Faerie is the easiest way to get there. There's a direct path to the land between. But you can also open a magical doorway from here, if you don't mind messing with dark magic."

The words slipped out before I could stop them. Only for Louis would I consider the use of dark magic. Jessa seemed to think about that suggestion. "That must have been how that supernatural smuggling ring worked," she finally said. "Dark magic was involved in setting up those fairy-tale houses that lured in the unsuspecting."

I knew about that also. Just because I chose to remain in my solitude didn't mean I wasn't somewhat up to date.

"Yes, it was definitely dark magic," I confirmed.

Jessa finally shook her head. "Louis wouldn't want us to mess with that sort of energy, not even to save him, so we better do this the old-fashioned way."

She knew him very well. Before I could think too much on it, I said, "I'll help you save him."

*Stupid, Tee.* I flinched then, when I realized I'd fallen into the habit of using my old nickname. I told everyone to call me Lizzie now, because Tee—shortened from my middle name, Teresa—died long ago. Being around Louis … it was messing with my head.

Jessa's smile brightened even more. "Thank you, we would really appreciate your help. Louis especially." Her eyes dropped to the form in the bed, her gaze running along his long limbs that dwarfed the double-sized mattress. Even in slumber he looked lethal. Dangerous.

I knew that Jessa was true mate to Braxton Compass, dragon shifter, leader of the shifter council in America, but there was definitely some sort of relationship between her and Louis. I found this curious, and I wanted to know how it had happened, because Louis had taken the same path as me for the past decades, avoiding close ties.

"How is it that you know Louis so well?" I asked.

She examined me closely, trying to discern deeper meaning, no doubt. But there was none. I was simply trying to piece together Louis's life now. The fact that he was even able to live a life when I'd continued to exist in exile kind of grated on my nerves. When did he stop hiding? Why hadn't I been told?

Jessa smiled then, her eyes on Louis once more. "He saved me when I was a baby, spelled my dragon mark so that I wouldn't be taken by the hunters. Then, when all hell broke loose with Larky, he stepped in and helped in every way. He also saved my children from being taken and used by a demon. I owe him *everything*." Her voice broke. "We would all be dead without his power and knowledge. He's one of my closest friends—family—and it is killing me to know that he's been trapped there this entire time while we've been screwing around with our heads up our asses."

I felt an instant kinship to Jessa. She reminded me of myself when I was younger. I'd been the headstrong one who cursed and snuck out, and sometimes read books about dark magic. Regina had been the perfect one, never causing a moment of upset for our parents. I'd been a poor replacement when she died.

Louis would be in good hands when he returned. He'd have the family he deserved. Now it was time to get it out of the way so I could get back to my ... existence.

"You should leave someone to guard him," I warned her as I moved toward the doorway. "Louis is old and powerful. He has plenty of enemies who would love to take advantage of his current state."

This time when her gaze dropped to the bed, anger creased her forehead. "No one in Stratford would dare! He saved us all from the demons. We owe him every-thing." She sucked in deeply, in what seemed like an attempt to calm herself. "But it doesn't hurt to be extra vigilant, in case an outsider breaks through our barriers or manages to trick their way inside. I'll get my father to stick around, assign some of the shifters to the case."

I nodded, satisfied with that. I knew Jonathon Lebron well, and I trusted him to do a damn good job of keeping Louis safe. We both left the hospital then, sparing Louis one more glance over our shoulders. The moment I was outside, I sucked in a deep breath. It was warm in Strat-ford, the climate much more hospitable than where I lived in Alaska. The snow was pretty peaceful though.

"You don't talk a lot, do you?" Jessa asked, distracting me from my inner monologue.

"I've been alone for ... too many years to count," I admitted, my voice soft. "You kind of just get used to the silence."

That wasn't completely true. I had three best friends up there, a group of supes who owned a hunting lodge near my cabin. The guys were all bear shifters, and they were noisy and fun and growly. They also encouraged my use of curse words, so I was back to my old ways. They were only at their cabin one week a month, though, so I was still alone a lot.

Speaking of, I better try to call them before they freaked out. They'd be due for their next trip really soon, and when they found my cabin empty, they'd definitely worry. I was always there.

"Why do you live alone?" Jessa asked in the blunt way of youth. Yeah, she made me feel every single one of my hundred-plus years.

"Because...." I cleared my throat. "Sometimes it's easier. Sometimes it hurts less being alone than losing people you love."

Even my bears... It was scary knowing how much I cared for them now. How much I looked forward to their visit every month. They'd wormed their way into my heart, and I again had something to lose. It was almost too scary to contemplate.

A warm hand wrapped around mine, squeezing tightly before releasing me again. I blinked at the shifter. "I'm so sorry," she murmured. "Louis was the same way when we first brought him into our world—shut off from everyone—but now he's family. Part of our pack. And he was much happier. At some point you have to make a choice—am I really living like this?"

"It's crazy," I said, unsure why I was sharing so much with her, "but I almost feel like I died when my sister did. Regina."

Jessa startled, her eyes growing wide. "Louis's mate?"

I nodded to answer the question in her tone. "Yes, they were together for five years before she was murdered."

"Holy fuck," she said, blinking at me. "How is it that none of us knew your sister was Louis's mate?"

I'd completely blindsided her with that. The funniest part was that Louis had been my best friend for years before he had anything to do with Regina. I'd been the idiot who had feared ruining the friendship, so I never pushed for anything more. Regina had no such qualms when she finally noticed how amazing Louis was. I hadn't been surprised when they fell for each other. But it had hurt. More than I thought anything could hurt. From then on, I'd just done my best to hide the attraction I'd always had for Louis. I never questioned their love, or that she was his chosen mate.

Even when it killed me.

"He blames himself," Jessa said as we started to walk again, faster this time.

I nodded. That was definitely no secret.

Thankfully, we seemed to have reached their home: a very impressive log cabin that bordered the back of the huge forests of Stratford. Conversation about Louis dried up, and I was grateful not to have to keep picking at old wounds.

Jessa led me inside, into a huge space they had set up as a living area. The doors and windows were open, allowing in cool breezes from the forests beyond. I could smell the wildflowers and the scent of our mother. Nature was everything to magic users. We communed with it all the time, and I missed this sort of greenery.

A large group of supes waited inside, and I forced my expression to go blank. Socializing was going to take some getting used to.

"Hey, everyone, gather around," Jessa said, waving her hands toward her face. "We're ready to head out now to save Louis, and I need to make sure we're all on the same page."

A devastatingly handsome shifter crossed to her. He had tousled dark hair, blue eyes, and dimples in both cheeks. He also had that look in his eyes that scary-powerful supes got, the one that said "do not mess with me or mine."

At the moment, though, he mostly seemed amused as he devoured Jessa with his gaze. "You know I love it when you're bossy," he rumbled, his arms wrapping around her as he pulled her closer.

Jessa's eyes closed as she sank against him, and I turned away because there was too much emotion there. It was almost painful watching that sort of true love.

"It's nice to see you again," Tyson Compass said, distracting me when he stepped closer. At his side was a tall, willowy redhead. She was beautiful, her eyes an arresting icy blue, her skin scattered with glittering pigment.

"The diamond princess," I breathed, unsure if I was actually seeing the truth.

She let out a tinkling laugh. "I prefer Grace," she said, her voice low and husky. "The whole *diamond princess* thing is going to take some getting used to."

"I thought you were a myth," I admitted. "Glad I was wrong about that, because keeping the shadows out of Faerie is a very important job."

Grace's expression turned confused as she tilted her head to the side. "You actually know about us?"

"Yeah, how the heck did you know about us?" I turned to find another beautiful woman stepping out from where she'd been perched in a nearby doorway. "We were a secret hidden for over twenty years."

"Ruby princess, I assume," I said, taking in her long

continue to practice and strengthen the natural bond that exists between you."

"I can feel them in my chest," Grace murmured. "Almost the same way I feel Tyson. Like there is a tangible connection between us."

"Sisters," Justice breathed, and this time there was no anger in her voice. She sounded like a lost little girl ... sad ... broken.

"Pack," Jessa chimed in. "Grace is our pack, and you're her sisters. We're family."

I could tell those words meant a lot to the four princesses, even the jaded Justice. Each of them turned shiny eyes on the unofficial leader of this pack. Jessa was decades younger than me, but I was pretty sure I could learn a thing or two from the wolf shifter.

The princesses' rainbow swirls changed then, the color intensifying as their energy grew stronger in the forest. "Do you feel our lands?" Grace murmured, her face slightly lifted as her eyes locked on the dance of color. "The jewels are calling to us."

"I feel it," Cam choked out. "It's ... everything."

She must have figured out how to connect then, because a portal burst to life, and it was different to a step-through in many ways. There was no swirling of energy. It was just a shimmer of rainbows, and on the other side was Faerie. Clear as anything. Like stepping through a reflection.

"That might be the most beautiful thing I've ever seen," I murmured. I could have opened a step-through to Faerie in a heartbeat, but then I would have missed this new magic, and there was nothing I loved more than the discovery of something new.

One by one, the pack crossed through the barrier to the other side. I was last, and as I reached out to run my hand across the shimmery strands of energy, I felt my body ease. The jeweled princesses were the keepers of something truly amazing. Original magic.

## 3

## ELIZABETH TERESA MONTGOMERY II

*I* hadn't been to Faerie for many years. Ironically enough, the last time I did come here was when Regina was killed. I'd had to escape. I'd been so angry; Louis had been the one to find me and bring me home, which, considering he was suffering from the loss of his mate, had been more shocking than anything else.

But he was selfless like that.

Always putting others first.

It was probably why he'd worked so well with Regina. She'd been the good girl, but deep down she had a need to be the center of attention. Needed all of the focus on her. A little selfish and self-centered. And Louis had indulged that side of her.

While I was dwelling on the past, the others had been moving around the area. The four princesses stood in front of their lands. Cam was staring out into an ocean, its waters lapping at her feet. Gretley appeared to be entranced by forests so green they almost looked unnatural. Justice was right at home with desert sands under her boots, her face lifted to the sky. And Grace had swirls of blue lighting her skin as she reached down to gather up handfuls of snow.

"Home," they all murmured together, somehow still linked.

"I know you all want to explore," Jacob said in that cocky yet reserved tone that was so fey in nature. "But we have to figure out how to save Louis first. Then you'll be free to embrace the jeweled lands."

With reluctance, they turned away. I could tell it was the last thing they wanted to do, but a sense of duty was strong with all of these supes. "Okay, so this portal to the land between ... anyone have a clue how we're supposed to open it?" Tyson ran a hand through his hair, tousling the shorter strands. "I mean, last time it was a demon-shadow team-up, but surely there's a way for us to do it that doesn't almost end the worlds."

"I thought the jeweled princesses could," Jessa suggested.

Knowing they probably wouldn't think to ask me, I said, "I can open one."

I was done with all of the delaying. I needed to save Louis so I could wipe our slate clean, then I could start living my life again. My trip back into the real world was showing me that it was time for me to step back into the land of the living.

Before any of them could argue, I moved into the center, onto the emblem of the four lands—the emblem that I could tell trapped the shadows—and lifted my hands to the sky. This spot here was a close link to the land between. Opening a doorway would be so easy that I barely even had to reach for the energy of the Faerie ley lines.

"We will have only seconds to cross," I warned them, holding on to my power for a moment longer. "Otherwise we risk the demons discovering the portal and using it to get back to Faerie."

"No problem," Braxton said, his voice grumbling. "Everyone will move their asses, or a dragon will be moving them."

Nervous chuckles all around, and then: "Wait!" Grace startled, her hands flinging to the sides. "We need the power of the jewels. I don't have any diamonds on me. Should we gather stones from our lands first?"

Gritting my teeth, because I was currently a conduit between two powerful energies—my own and Faerie's, I nodded my head. "Yes, sure, but please hurry. This is not the most pleasant of sensations."

I heard Tyson clear his throat, and I turned to see him nearby. "Are you holding a ley line right now?" he asked, blinking at me. "Like ... just holding the energy and not directing it anywhere?"

I nodded, amusement spiking through my mind. There was so much fascination in his focused gaze. No wonder he'd managed to break Louis's record as the youngest sorcerer. He was determined and strong, and power definitely intrigued him. Not to mention the magical bond with his brothers that was akin to that of the jeweled princesses'. Unique.

"You'll learn how to hold the energy of a world," I told him slowly, keeping my breaths even. "Eventually. Don't try it until you're ready. I can see your magic is a little ragged at the moment. You've pushed yourself too far and too fast."

He nodded, the masculine lines of his face defining further. "I had no choice, it was level up or the worlds would end, but I'm ready to slow my sorcerer ascension a little now. I have a lot to learn."

I swallowed hard, and my voice sounded huskier than usual. "You have no better teacher than Louis. He taught me everything I know, guiding me in the early days when I was strong and ambitious and a little too greedy for power. Once you have him back, then you'll have your best asset at learning power control."

Tyson *almost* looked like he wanted to argue with me before he let out a small huff of air. "As much as I hate to admit it, that arrogant sorcerer is pretty fucking powerful. Still, I'm almost certain I could best him if I set my mind to it."

I internally laughed, and my amusement was no doubt clearly on my face.

"Ignore him," Grace said, slightly breathless after sprinting back from the diamond lands. "He's confident to the point of arrogance."

"All of the Compasses are," Mischa piped up. "It's one of their more ... and less ... endearing traits."

My chuckle was strangled as more of Faerie's power shocked me. "I'm used to men like that," I rasped out. "Their attitude changes when I slap them down with a little power."

Jessa laughed out loud, a tinkle across the Faerie air. "That's my favorite thing to do. Only I use my fists."

"It really is her favorite pastime," Braxton said drily.

I was relieved to see that the other princesses had

returned also, and each held a fist-sized stone. "How did you get the stones?" I gritted out, mentally preparing to open the doorway.

"We seem to be able to ask our lands for things, and they deliver like the best kind of Jeeves," Justice told me from nearby. I had no idea what a Jeeves was, but I guessed it was some sort of human reference.

"I'm opening the doorway now," I said, letting the power unfurl from me. I had thought I was doing a pretty good job controlling the level of energy, but a lot more than expected burst from me, creating a massive step-through.

I was rusty. I needed to use my abilities more—I'd practically been living like a human over the last few decades.

"Go," I shouted, already hurrying forward. My long hair streamed out behind me as I picked up the pace.

Curses ripped from me as I closed in on the portal. I'd always planned the step-through to be large enough for everyone to run through at the same time, but this one was at least double the size needed. That level of power would draw demon attention. We had to hurry.

Even though I'd managed to take off first, they'd all caught me quickly. Short legs were a curse at times. As I'd planned, we hit the portal at the same moment; the journey across was fast and bumpy. As my feet landed on the hard, unforgiving terrain of the land between, I immediately sucked my power back inside, hiding it away.

The other side was dark and cold, so I sent up a few dim balls of magic, doing a quick head count. Four Compasses. Four jeweled princesses. Two Lebron sisters.

I shut the doorway down in the same instant, relieved that I didn't feel the presence of any dark demon energy.

Not yet anyway.

"Time to find Louis," Jessa said, her voice low and determined. "The demons are going to wish they never touched my brother."

"Thankfully, we have dragon fire," Braxton said confidently. "Because I know of nothing else that could deter them."

All eyes turned on me, and then everyone moved in closer to form a tight circle under my lights. I realized that they were waiting for me to confirm that there was no other weapon we could use against the demons. Part of me was surprised and grateful that they already respected my power and knowledge, even before I'd really done anything to prove myself to them.

It spoke of a confidence they had in themselves, because otherwise they'd be trying to do this all without any help. Just to prove they could.

Keeping my voice to a whisper and my senses on high alert, I quickly said, "There is a spell I can use on lower-level demons. They'll be repelled across this world, unable to return for a long time." I swallowed hard. "But for the upper-level demons, like the one Louis banished ... I've never known anyone to actually best them in a battle unless they were bonded to a supe. Defeat the supe and you have a chance to banish them back to this world. There's a split second of vulnerability."

"That's what Louis did," Mischa said, her voice sounding hoarse. "But for some reason his soul went along with it."

"Which demon was it?" I asked, realizing there was a chance I'd know the name.

"Davind," Tyson replied. "He was insanely powerful. His energy literally cut through ours."

Swallowing roughly, I tried to steady my breathing. "Davind is one of their leaders. There's almost none as powerful as he is. Louis knew this. He has fought that particular demon before, and he knew...."

That there was no other way. Davind didn't steal Louis's soul and take it back. Louis attached himself to the demon and then used his energy to send them both back to the land between.

"He knew what would happen?" Jessa breathed. "He knew he would be taken to the land of demons, and he still chose that path."

"He chose to save us all." Mischa was crying now, tears silently tracking down her cheeks, barely visible in the low light. "To save our babies."

"Yes," I confirmed, not at all surprised. My feelings for Louis were hard to define, because there was a lot of anger and pain intertwined with all of the millions of good memories, but I would never deny the pureness and light of his soul. He was one of the best supernaturals I'd ever known, and just because he'd broken my heart didn't make that any less true.

"So how do we find him," Jessa whispered, leaning in even closer. The wild scent of shifter washed across my senses, and despite our current dire circumstances, a flicker of joy at being back with supernaturals hit me.

I was so ready to return to this world.

"I'm going to track him," I said quietly. "We will have to move quickly because demons will be drawn to our energy. This world is dead, the ley lines depleted to the point where I almost can't feel them. So we're going to stand out."

The three dragons especially.

I eyed the fourth Compass, the huge vampire who apparently didn't have a dragon yet. But I could see what a lot of them wouldn't be able to; his dragon was there, just under the surface.

Maximus regarded me while I watched him, amusement flickering across his dark eyes. "What are you seeing?" he finally asked.

"You have the energy of a dragon," I murmured. "It's not released yet, but it will come in time."

My words seemed to please him. He stood even taller, towering over Mischa, who was at his side. Wasting no more time on that, I focused instead on finding Louis. His energy was more familiar to me than almost anyone's, and I found him with ease. "Got him," I said, locking my own energy onto his.

I got a wisp of power in return, and worry bloomed with full force in my mind. He was weak.

"Hang on, I'm going to open a step-through. We don't have any time to waste," I said, before reaching for the stores of my power inside. It was odd using my own power only, but there was no other choice here. I just had to be careful not to use too much, in case we had to fight.

Darkness washed across my senses just as the doorway swirled into existence. "Demons," I bit out harshly, before sending out a shield to delay the evil entities heading our way. "Move. Now."

I let them go through first, until there was only

Braxton and me left. "You go," he said, "I'll keep the demons at bay."

I shook my head. "No, you will be overwhelmed in seconds. I'm holding them back right now, but there's literally a thousand of them closing in on us. They like to stay close to the portal of Faerie. Close to a land of energy."

Braxton grumbled, his huge chest lifting. "Then we go together. No one gets left behind on my watch."

I knew it was bothering him to be here while the rest of his pack was on the other side of my step-through. I felt the same way, so I just nodded and reached out to link my arm through his. That way I knew we'd both make it through and I could shut the doorway down before the demons broke through the last of my barrier.

When we popped out on the other side, there were multiple breaths of relief. "You scared me a little," Grace admitted, moving forward. "I wasn't sure you were going to make it through."

"Lizzie was holding the demons back," Braxton told her. "I had to make sure she didn't get left behind."

Without seeing our surroundings, I shut down the step-through, making sure nothing followed us. When I finally got a chance to look around, I had to blink at the unnatural brightness a few hundred yards away from us.

"Circus of Souls, I'm going to assume," Justice said, her eyes locked on the flashing and zigzagging illumination. "This is where Louis is supposed to be?"

"That's where they said he was," Jessa bit out. "Let's go pay them a visit." Determination creased her brow. "I'm ready to have him back. I need him back."

Everyone moved closer together, keeping an eye out

as we started to walk in the direction of the lights. I could feel Louis's waning energy with each step we took toward that place.

Instinctively, I knew one thing for sure.

We were running out of time.

## 4

## LOUIS

*A* running stream of black-and-white images flashed through my mind. I was not controlling them, and each one sent inky spirals of darkness through me. This was their new form of torture, and for the first time I wasn't sure I would make it through without breaking. Regina ... her eyes wide and filled with laughter as she ran from me. There was a field of wildflowers just near their house. She would spend hours dashing through them, picnic basket and rug in hand for when she grew tired and wanted to lie back and stare at the clouds overhead. I always knew I could find her out there when she disappeared.

*Wait ... no.* That was wrong. It wasn't Regina who loved the wildflowers.

It was *Tee.*

I had no idea why the images of Elizabeth Teresa—Tee to me—were being confused in the demons' walk down memory lane. Because they were sisters? Was my mind reaching the end of its limits?

Was I starting to fade?

I'd never confused Tee and Regina before. Outside of them being sisters, they had very little else in common. Regina was tall and broad, lots of curves and muscles. She was loud and funny and dramatic. She was a good girl, always following the rules, but she had a cheeky side as well. She also loved attention, always wanting people to watch her and appreciate her gifts. Tee was none of those things. Quiet and powerful, she commanded attention even when she didn't want it. She was also beyond kind and smart; she'd been my first real friend. She had saved me from the lonely existence that probably would have destroyed any slice of good inside of me.

And I'd lost her too.

The wildflowers disappeared then, as did my maudlin memories, and another set of images appeared.

*No!*

They'd finally found the wound at my center.

The moment I came home to find Regina lifeless, her blood and energy ripped from her body ... nothing more than a shell. The vivacious, funny, headstrong magic user I had loved was gone.

I hadn't been there to save her.

I'd been busy with my sorcerer duties. With being the strongest mage there ever was. With being the best.

I should have been home.

It was one of my greatest regrets, and it hurt like nothing I'd ever felt to see her again. The demons made it so real. I could smell the copper of her blood. Taste the remaining resonance of her fear and pain.

A guttural roar burst from me, and since I hadn't made a sound for a very long time, that was a win for the demons. Regina's body disappeared in my mind's eye and I tried to breathe through my pain. There was no time to regroup though; the next scene was Tee stumbling into the house to find me crouched by her sister. She had screamed and screamed, and then she took off. I left Regina and chased her, because she was all I had left in the world.

Together we had mourned, and then I had lost her too.

"You're going to lose her permanently," the demon hissed at me, its translucent body drifting around me. "The one who holds your soul."

Tee's face was burned into my brain, and a dull roar in my head was making it hard to think clearly. I found myself asking, "What are you talking about?" My voice was rusty from not being used. "The one who held my soul is already dead."

Chilling laughter from another demon. I couldn't tell them apart when they swirled in and around each other like this. There were at least twenty of them surrounding me this torture session, closing in, their coldness seeping into my essence.

"Wrong," it replied. "You're so very wrong."

I jerked on the chains, my movements slow, but determination to reach one of these bastards was filling me. If I could get my hands on them, I might be able to absorb their energy and refuel my own. This was a last-ditch option, because the darkness in a demon's soul had to go somewhere, and that somewhere would be right into my soul, but I was desperate. They must have sensed that– they were smart enough to hover just out of my reach.

"You're very weak now," a demon said, swirling to just

beyond my fingertips. "Very weak. Would you like to make a deal?"

Rock bottom had come and gone long ago. The fact that I was considering absorbing a demon's energy told me everything I needed to know about my mental state. But still I would not make a deal. I could not. If my body and power were returned to Earth with a demon riding shotgun, then the world was over. As much as I wanted to end my captivity and suffering, I could not do that to the world. Absorbing some of their energy was different to allowing them to use my body and power on Earth. The former should still allow me some control until I could release the darkness. The latter would strip my free will from me.

The swirls of demons around me stopped moving then, and I wondered what had distracted them. Less than ten seconds later, I straightened as familiar energy brushed against me. *Fuck.* Everything inside of me went icy cold. Jessa and her pack were here, their bright energy like a beacon in this dead land. They had arrived in the land between, and while part of me was grateful to know they hadn't given up on me, I really wished they had. Now I was going to have to watch them perish because I was too weak to save them.

The only positive in my current situation, stuck in the center of a very well-lit circle of hellfire, was that no upper-level demons were inside with me at the moment. These lower-levels would be deterred by dragons—their fire could destroy them—so my family had that one chance.

The fires soared higher then as the demons fed energy into the magical flame. Hellfire would burn a soul and physical body to dust in a fraction of a second. It cost them a lot of energy to keep it powered, but it was essential when they had to unchain us for certain physical tortures or when we were moved. The fire was the only thing keeping us from escaping when we had those few moments of freedom.

And it would stop my family from getting to me.

Powerful gusts of air started buffeting the flames, and icy tendrils of strong magic brushed across my soul. My senses were dull without my body, but I could still feel the difference in air temperature. A roar drew the mass of dark demons closer to the center of the flames, and they started to rise up, until they were hovering near the stone ceiling.

As the familiar energy of my family drew closer, the darkness that lay under my sorcery energy started to swell. Soon it boiled and churned within me. The light I used to fight the sorcery darkness was almost gone— whatever the demons had done to me since I got here and the loss of my normal power and resilience had all but obliterated my control. The final straw was possibly losing my only family.

One demon had remained close, and in its distraction —watching the others—it drifted into my space. My hands brushed through the specter, and I didn't hesitate to connect our energy.

Everything went misty then and I embraced it, allowing the power of this demon to fill me. I was basically draining it, which was very different to allowing it to possess me. If I'd been in my body, I'd never have been able to do this, but since I was only a soul as well, it worked.

As more of the mist filled me, rational thought faded. I didn't care. This was what I needed to save them. As I let more of the darkness rise up through my soul, it released a power and energy that I hadn't felt in a long time. Light was stronger, but darkness was willing to do anything to succeed, and it was not weakened by this world. Or by demons.

My strength returned.

Once I'd drained the demon, I threw it away, the wispy remains of its power flickering on and off. My soul started to expand; the chains holding me rattled as my energy destroyed them. In this moment, I couldn't remember why I'd always shied away from darker magic. That had been a stupid rule to follow, because now I'd have the power ... the strength ... to make sure that no one was ever taken from me again.

I would be a god. If I'd been this strong when Regina was alive, she'd still be here with me. Another roar burst from me, deep and guttural, and echoed around the fire pit with enough force that if I'd been in my physical body my eardrums would have burst. Silence descended over the entire area; the demons even stopped their chattering to move closer to me,

The final clank of my chains hitting the ground was extra loud in the silence.

"How?" a demon hissed, rushing toward me. It hovered over the one I'd drained for a beat, and then flames appeared within the center of its dark cloud. It was one of their favorite weapons: a cloud of pain.

Only I was not vulnerable any longer.

The darkness of my new energy pushed forward, and I let it go free. The demon dissolved in an instant, whatever fire it had been holding going with it. The others halted their downward trajectory and immediately tried to go in the opposite direction, sensing their impending doom.

I gave them exactly what they expected. Instant death.

The remaining souls in here belonged to supernaturals, and they were all chained down. Each cried out weakly, asking me to free them, but it was not in my interest to bother. I didn't need them; therefore there was no point in wasting time or energy on them.

They should think themselves lucky I didn't require their energy to escape, because I would have just taken it. It was my right to take whatever I needed.

Everything was mine now.

## 5

## ELIZABETH TERESA MONTGOMERY II

*M*y focus on Louis's energy was so strong that I barely noticed anything else around me. The only time I was remotely distracted was when we encountered small pockets of demons. The closer we got to the light, the more demons there were. But with three dragons and my own power, we were easily able to overcome them. I had no idea what dragon fire did to them, but it certainly made them scatter when it started to spew in their direction.

Eventually we found ourselves huddled on the edge of a large stone building. Turned out those unnaturally bright lights were hiding a bunch of buildings. "He's in here," I murmured as we moved closer, just on the edge of a section where the light didn't touch.

"There's a lot of energy here," Braxton replied in a whisper of husky tones. "A lot more than I've felt since we arrived. I'm going to shift again."

"Should we all shift?" Jacob asked, pushing back a few strands of white-blond hair.

"Three dragons is going to draw a lot of attention," Jessa said, her gaze landing on mine. "But ... maybe that's what we should be doing. Distract the demons with dragons, so the rest of us can sneak in and save Louis...?"

I thought on it for a moment. "The idea has merit," I said with a nod. "I can't think of anything with less risk. The dragons are at least very resistant to dark energy, and their fire scares the demons."

Tyson's face darkened. "I'm not comfortable leaving you all here without the power of our dragons. What happens if there's an entire army of demons inside? You'll be dead or possessed before you know it."

"We're not without our own skills," Grace reminded him, and of all people, he paid the most attention to her. "The four of us carry jewels and powers from our lands, Lizzie is as strong as Louis, and you know better than to discount Jess and Misch."

Maximus snorted. "What about me?" he grumbled. "Am I just the token guy in this situation?"

Mischa reached out and patted his thick biceps. "Don't worry, hon, I'll keep you safe."

He shook his head. "Our women definitely rule this pack. But let's not forget that I have some skills."

Grace waved a hand in his direction. "Yes, we also have Max and his ... skills."

I wanted to chuckle at their gentle mocking, because the very powerful men they were mated to probably did need to be pulled down a few pegs at times, but this was not the sort of situation for laughter.

Tyson, Braxton, and Jacob all wore the same expression, none of them happy that our plan included separating, but they didn't argue again. No doubt they were hoping that in the end they would be the ones in the most danger.

The three of them stepped back and quickly shucked their clothing off. No one bothered to look away; nudity was not a big deal in the supe world. I was too old to give a shit about seeing a few guys' junks—the fact I was even saying the word "junk" told me I'd been hanging around my Alaskan shifter friends for far too long—once you'd seen some junk, you'd pretty much seen it all.

Well, sorta. The Compasses were pretty impressive in their nakedness—even if they were years too young for me, and all mostly in true mate bonds—and they were even more impressive when they turned into massive dragons.

Jessa let out a wistful sigh. "Some days I miss Josephina so much it's actually painful. I miss having her close to talk to, and her power and protection. Especially now that I have children, being able to protect my pack seems more important than ever."

I couldn't even imagine a loss like that, something so fundamental to yourself. No wonder Jessa was so strong and resilient. She might be young, but she'd been through a lot.

Mischa and Grace wrapped their arms around her, and the three remained close as they watched the giant beasts rise up into the air. The lights that had been swirling around the circus turned in their direction. Braxton, a black-and-blue-scaled dragon, roared before flames spewed from his jaw. His wings flapped lazily, sending plumes of dust across the arid landscape. The other two flanked him, one a sleek green beast with scales that sparkled with an extra oomph of intensity, while the other was tawny and broad, and the glint of intensity in its large eyes told me that Tyson was just as determined in dragon form.

If not more so.

Three plumes of fire filled the sky, and more roars from the beasts. The lights were now all moving in their direction, which allowed us to creep forward in the shadows. Demons poured from the circus, heading toward them. They seemed to think that in large numbers they might have a shot against the dragon flame.

"How many demons exist here?" Justice whispered, ducking down as we hurried forward. "Like ... are there millions?"

"No way to really tell," I said, sliding under an open doorway of a nearby tent-like structure. "I would guess, maybe ... a hundred thousand. The numbers increase as more supes ... and humans ... find their way to the dark side. This land will not be able to contain them all one day."

Cam shivered, her hands tightening on the sapphire stone she had clutched close to her chest. "They scare me," she admitted in a whisper. "I have nightmares about being taken over by the darkness that we fought back in Faerie. Of falling like Grace did."

It sounded like she'd been holding that fear inside. She looked astonished that she had admitted it out loud. Gretley reached out and wrapped an arm around her, pulling her close. "I have the same nightmare," she murmured into the top of Cam's head. "I'm not sure I'll ever be able to close my eyes and not see that shadow again."

My heart ached for all of them. I'd been young when

my life fell apart too, but at least they had each other. These close family ties would help them get through it all.

"It's only been a few days," I said softly. "Give yourself time. Trauma does not heal overnight."

Or even in a few decades. But it did get easier to live with.

We were all inside a huge tent now, and it was hotter in here than it had been anywhere else in this land. I continued to follow the pull of Louis's power. Sticking to the shadows, I kept my senses alert for any demon presence, but it felt like this area was clear. That was, until we found ourselves on the edge of a red flame, one that reached all the way to the ceiling of this "tent."

The wall of flames was different to any other fire I'd seen before. It was smooth, no flickering or surging, and it circled around something. The heat it emitted was intense, and whatever was inside the circle with Louis was dark. Like ... fifty demons dark. "It feels like Louis is being held in here," I said. "But there are also a lot of demons inside."

Running my hands close to the fire, I said, "I'm going to try and blast a small hole through it so that we can enter."

"Are you sure he's in there?" Maximus asked.

I nodded. "Yep, definitely."

To double-check, I walked the full circle of the flames and found no other trace of Louis outside of this spot. The others followed me until we ended up back in the place we started. "He's definitely inside, and the darkness I feel in there is growing."

"I can feel it too," Grace choked out. "It's just like the

shadow energy back on Faerie." She lifted the crystal to chest height. The diamond was starting to glow in a way it hadn't since she picked it up from her land. "The jewels are responding."

"Could there be a shadow here?" Cam asked, her eyes wide.

No one answered, because we really didn't know what was inside. Shadows had started as upper-level demons, so while the one inside might not be exactly like the shadow she had fought in Faerie, it didn't mean its power wasn't similar. And there might even be more than one in there.

"We have no choice," Jessa said with force. "We've left Louis too long as it is; who knows what he's been suffering here at the hands of these demons. If he's on the other side, I will not walk away now. I don't care what we have to fight to get him back."

"This is why we had to be here," Gretley said, straightening. I was starting to see that she was quiet and brave. "The jewels are designed to fight darkness. It's literally what our people have been doing for a very long time. We're the best defense against the upper-level demons."

"We're not trained though," Cam reminded her, still looking fragile and scared. "We have no freaking idea what we're doing."

Justice shook out her hair, the red and orange of the fire reflecting off the white strands. "We need to stick together and go on instinct. It's helped us defeat evil in the past, and it will help us again."

Her reassurance seemed to instill a sliver of confidence in the others, and I didn't think they even realized it, but they all moved a little closer to one another, needing the comfort of their bond. Jessa met my gaze and smiled. "We got this," she told me.

I was old enough to know that too much confidence could be lethal. You went in cocky, you didn't plan enough, you got dead. But ... we didn't really have another option. Louis needed us. He was right there, and I was channeling Jessa when I said, "Let's do this. The demons are going down, and Louis is coming home with us."

As soon as we freed him from whatever they were using to hold him here, his soul would return to its body. It was not meant to exist here; it still had a vessel.

"Well, if you're ready, I'm going to break through this flame," I said, gathering almost all of the energy I had left inside. Had to save some to return us home. "It's probably going to drain me considerably, but know I will do everything I can to assist you with whatever waits on the other side."

I'd never worked with this sort of flame before, but I had an idea what it was. Hellfire. Designed to burn souls as well as the flesh, it was no doubt the very thing keeping Louis trapped here. I closed my eyes to focus.

*Lestinae fortuna legresia momentum.* I let the spell swirl around my mind, and my power surged up, rising from my center. *Resista flamina.*

My skin grew hot as my body vibrated. My parents had always joked that I was too small to contain so much magical essence, that one day it would burst my skin, especially if I ever released it all without the help of a ley line to filter it.

Looked like we were about to find out.

Maximus stepped in front of Mischa, pulling Jessa

into his side just as the spell reached its full potential, crashing out of me with the force of a tsunami. The jeweled princesses lifted their stones, and light shone out in a protective glow around them. My arms shook as I struggled to keep the focus of my spell. I needed all of it to stay on the flames. It was the only way I could guarantee to split the fire.

For a brief moment I didn't think it had worked, because the red remained unbroken, and as sweat beaded on my forehead I shook with the force of maintaining the power. Then, hope infused in me when the smallest of gaps appeared.

"You got this, Lizzie," Jessa yelled, her voice barely penetrating through the magic roaring around me. "Don't give up."

I wouldn't give up, but I also wasn't near a ley line. Eventually my own magic would run out, and if the wall wasn't parted by then, we'd never get to Louis.

"Once it's open," I gritted out, projecting my voice, "get in there straight away. We won't have much time."

My voice sounded labored, and I pushed myself harder because I needed it done.

The fire split further and further, inch by inch, until there was a doorway big enough for me. Of course, outside of Cam, I was the smallest one there, and I couldn't risk this fire touching any of them. It was not a burn supes could heal from.

I dug even deeper, searching for hidden strength. I could do this, I knew I could do it, but before I could release any more energy, a shadow darted across the entrance I'd created.

I froze.

Demons. Shit. Shit. They were already coming for us.

I'd figured they wouldn't even notice us until we were inside, but I hadn't taken into account how much time it would take to break the hellfire. An inky energy, darker than any I'd ever felt, pushed through the doorway, blasting all of us back. I used magic to stop myself from hitting the ground, skidding on my boots instead. My eyes immediately shot to the fire, and I could have cried when I saw it whole and unbroken.

All that work for nothing. We hadn't gotten to Louis, and I'd only succeeded in letting out an upper-level demon. We were now in very real danger, and I wasn't sure I had the energy to break the wall again.

Before I could worry about that though, there was a demon to deal with.

I stayed still, half hidden in the shadows, my eyes the only things moving as I tried to track the darkness. It felt like it was everywhere, and so freaking strong that my teeth were actually aching from the energy.

"Lizzie!" Jessa shouted. "Are you okay?"

"Yes," I called back just as quickly. "There's an upper-level demon in here, so be aware."

A specter appeared in the center of the space, and a dozen or so lights focused on it. The gasp fell from my lips before I could stop it, and I swear my heart stuttered out of rhythm.

"Louis?" I choked out.

He might have been in soul form, but it was clearly the sorcerer. I would recognize him anywhere, even mostly translucent and coated in swirling darkness. Jessa and Mischa rushed to my side, both of them reaching for me. I grasped their hands, pulling them back.

"It's Louis?" Jessa asked, squinting as she tried to see through the inkiness that surrounded him.

I nodded, swallowing hard. "Yes. That's Louis's soul. And—"

"Something happened to him," Maximus bit out, his body growing larger. He vamped out, his fangs appearing as his eyes darkened. "He's demon touched."

I shook my head. "No, no, that's not right. He isn't demon touched. He has no body to be demon touched. It's something else..."

Louis laughed then, and it brought every hair on my body to attention as a shiver ran down my spine. Holy gods. This was bad. This was really bad.

"My family," Louis said, waving his arms in our direction. "Here to save me."

Jessa released me, taking a small step toward him. "Louis?" she questioned again.

Some of the joviality slid from his face. "You don't recognize your own brother?" His tone was harder, the darkness swirling higher.

"You're covered in what looks like a demon, dude," Jessa shot back, no fear in her tone. I could tell this was stressing her out, though. Her nails appeared to be actually drawing blood in her palms. "What happened to you?"

Louis laughed again. This time it was a roar of sound as he sent power flying around the room. "I embraced the dark magic inside. You know all magic users have it, but we are taught to suppress it because they want us weak."

*Yeah, no, that wasn't the reason, Louis.* It was because magic users turned into evil assholes without morality or empathy when they embraced the darkness of their magic.

His eyes met mine, and it almost looked like flames flickered across his face. "What are you doing here, *Elizabeth*?"

The anger in his voice was real, and it sparked my own anger. I had never done anything to Louis that warranted his hatred of me, but still, he'd cut me out of his life like I was nothing. Like we hadn't shared so much, lost someone we both loved, and somehow made it to the other side.

He'd just cut me out.

"I'm here to help save your sorry ass," I all but shouted at him, losing control of my emotions. He did this to me every damned time. "Your soul wouldn't have gotten out of the fire if I hadn't spelled it apart."

He laughed again before zooming forward, his speed so rapid that it was only an instant before he was towering over me. For the first time, I felt true fear as he stared down at me.

"I could have split that fire without breaking a sweat. I was just curious to see if you could do it." He shot me a cold look. "I never expected to see you again. The bringer of bad memories."

His words triggered something in me, a deep-seated fear that had held me immobile for years. "You wish I'd died instead of Regina?" I choked out, tears burning the back of my throat and eyes. "You've always wished that."

I waited for him to confirm it, but he just sneered. "I'm ready to return to my body now," he told me softly. "And I'll finally have the strength befitting a sorcerer of my level. I'll finally be strong enough to ensure that no one will be taken from me again. Ever." His whisper turned insidious. "If you think you can best me, then bring your A game. Because I'm stronger than I've ever been."

Fear held me as I tried to process what was happening here. How had Louis gone dark like this? I didn't understand. The natural light of all mages kept our darker instincts under control, and Louis, more than anyone, was filled with light energy.

What did the demons do to him? How did they break him like this?

Jessa opened her mouth to say something, but Louis was so focused on me he didn't see it. Before she could speak, there was a *pop*, and the specter that was Louis disappeared.

I cried out, falling to my knees. Mischa dropped down next to me. "What just happened?" she asked, reaching for my arm.

My chest heaved as I fought for breath. "Louis ... he's embraced dark magic," I said in a strangled voice. "We all have dark in our magic. Yin and yang. It's important for balance, but we are taught from a young age to focus on the light, which is naturally a little stronger. Whatever happened here, Louis has lost his balance. He has embraced the dark side."

"Where is he now?" Maximus asked, his voice thundering.

"Back," I whispered, forcing myself to my feet. I felt weak and fragile, like a strong breeze would just carry me away. "He's gone back to his body, because there was nothing more holding his soul here."

"With a demon?" Jessa screamed. "He's gone back with a demon in his soul still?"

"No..." I shook my head. "There's no actual demon inside of him. This is Louis's own darkness, the energy that had always been in his soul. In his magic." They weren't magic users, they didn't understand. This was not an evil entity that we could exorcise from Louis; this was his own power.

Jessa looked confused, but Grace, who was nearby with her sisters, nodded. "Yes, it's true. I was worse than most because I had an actual shadow inside of me, but there's always darkness in magic. It's just usually beaten back by the light in our souls."

"Louis's soul was hurt, tortured, broken down in so many ways that the light dimmed." I realized the truth of this even as I spoke it out loud. "And now he's back in Stratford."

"We have to get back too." Jessa was already moving. "We left our entire town there, vulnerable to Louis."

There was a noise nearby, and I spun around, prepared to battle, but it was only the other Compasses. "Jessa already told me everything," Braxton said. "What can we expect from this dark Louis?"

I shook my head. "I have no idea. I've never seen a sorcerer as powerful as he is go dark. I'm guessing something akin to Kristoff."

"But he was demon touched," Tyson said, his eyes blazing with a mix of color. "Louis doesn't have a demon inside."

"Kristoff didn't start demon touched, though," I reminded them. "He started by embracing the darkness. Once they're demon touched, they're completely unreachable. Louis ... he should be more reasonable. Nothing is controlling him yet. It's still Louis, just a Louis who is easier to anger and hungry for power and energy."

"We have to get back to Stratford. Now!" Jessa all but yelled. "Can you open a step-through back there, Lizzie?"

I was tapped out, my energy fizzing around inside of me with that buzz of fatigue that followed overuse, but I had to try. "I'll do my best."

Demons appeared in the doorway then, a large group of them judging by the power.

"We'll keep them back." Braxton's voice was already deepening as he started to shift. "Just get us back to Stratford."

"Us too," Justice said, and she and her sisters raised their jewels and the light washed over us. Protectively.

I nodded and closed my eyes. I could do this; I had to do this, because Louis was capable of anything right now, and once he was back with the ley lines, he would be near unstoppable.

Just as I reached for the last of my energy inside, I heard Grace whisper to Tyson. "Has a sorcerer ever come back from this kind of darkness?"

He hesitated before he said, "I've never heard of it. Unless we can figure out how to bring him back, we'll have no choice but to kill Louis."

That was the truth I had been hiding from since the moment I realized the dark energy was my oldest friend. And enemy.

I was going to have to kill Louis.

## 6

## LOUIS

*T*he journey back to my body was easy. The vessel had weakened in my soul's absence, but the moment we reunited, power rushed through every cell and filled my center. Returning to the vessel gave me some clarity, knowledge of what I needed to do now that I was back and at full power.

As I rose from the bed, flinging off the magical attachments that must have been trying to keep me functioning, I ignored the shocked look of the shifter at my bedside and clothed myself in long dark robes. Not my usual attire, but I was not my usual self any longer.

As I strode from the room, there was a gasp from the front desk. "Louis!" a dark-skinned, long-legged healer cried. She was beautiful, but did not have enough power to interest me. "You're awake. Oh my gods. We've been waiting so long for you to—"

I waved my hand and cut her babbling off midsentence. Her eyes widened as she stared mutely at me. "Yes, I have awakened. I need you now to run off and tell the rest of the town that we will be having a meeting. In the main hall. I want to see every single face in twenty minutes or I will come and find them. And they won't like what happens if I have to do that."

Her eyes widened. The old me, the weaker version of me, never spoke to others this way. I was standoffish but respectful—which had gotten me nowhere. It was time for me to be the sorcerer and leader I was always meant to be. It was time to take Stratford—and America—back. The Compasses weren't here. Again they'd left this town to fend for itself. It was time to usurp those bastards and take back what should have stayed mine.

As I walked from the room I released the magic holding the healer's tongue and was happy to see she had already picked up the phone. Everyone would be at the town meeting, I already knew that, and while I waited for them to gather, I needed to stop by my old home.

I had something there to grab, something I required to bring myself, and the rest of our world, to full power.

A beautiful face flashed across my mind, and with it came a rising swell of darkness inside of me. *Elizabeth.* I hadn't seen her for years. I'd thought I would never see her again after our last fight. What the hell was she doing here? Why would she come back now?

She was just here to destroy me again. The demons had known she was a weakness for me, and weaknesses could not be tolerated.

*Fuck.* She had looked exactly the same. Hair like spun gold as it trailed down her back. Fire in her shimmery silver eyes. She'd always been able to cut me down with one look, and I'd always let her get away with it, but no more. She'd better stay out of my way, or I would make her.

*You wished I died.* Her words, designed to appeal to my softer side, her pain so clear as she uttered them. But it was too late for that. I didn't care anymore.

I could never forget though, that while Elizabeth might be one of the most beautiful creatures I'd ever seen, she was also one of the deadliest. Her power was strong, and it compared to mine, something most didn't know. I would not underestimate her.

Not for one second.

Maybe it was time to show my little Elizabeth that there was someone she should fear. And that someone was me.

## 7

## ELIZABETH TERESA MONTGOMERY II

*I* managed to get the step-through to Faerie open, but it cost me the last of my energy to do so. Jacob practically carried me across as we followed the others. Braxton was last through, sending flames out behind him before he shifted from dragon to human. I shut the step-through down before anything sinister could follow. Then the princesses did their thing and got us back home.

After being in the dark for so long, the light of Earth was almost blinding, and the energy here was overwhelming. In the same way as when senses were cut off briefly before returning, I suddenly felt everything so strongly. I struggled to free myself from Jacob, collapsing to the ground, where I lay breathing in nature, absorbing the energy of the ley lines as they filled my well of power again.

"Are you okay, Lizzie?" Jessa asked, her voice low, sounding like she was hovering just above my head.

"I'm fine," I said, voice muffled. "Just communing with nature."

"She's filling her energy," Tyson and Grace said at the same time.

As more of my power returned, some of the hopelessness I'd been feeling faded away. I wasn't exactly optimistic as I got to my feet, but I also wasn't ready to just give up.

"What do we do now?" Braxton stared at me, his eyes shimmering with yellow. "Our borders have not been touched since we left, which means Louis is still inside. Somewhere."

I sent out my own senses, giving the town a quick once-over. "There's a congregation of supes in the main hall," I told them. "Louis is on the other side of Stratford though ... near a waterfall. But I can sense no death and destruction, so he's containing himself."

"He's at his house," Jessa said, turning to her mate. "What could he be doing there?"

"He might be contained now, but it'll only take one issue, right?" Grace interrupted.

I nodded. He was a bomb waiting to go off right now.

Grace turned to her jeweled sisters. "I think we should go back to Faerie. If anyone knows how to combat darkness, it's our people there. Maybe they'll have some insights that will help us save Louis?"

I personally thought that was a great idea. Not all darkness was the same, and the shadows were not what had Louis in their grasp, but the basic concept of the energy he was now possessed by was the same as that of the demons.

"I'll go with you," Tyson said to Grace.

She shook her head, reaching up and placing both of her palms against his face. "I want you with me more than anything, but the danger is here. You need to stay and keep our family safe. You need to keep Stratford safe." She stood on her tiptoes and pressed a kiss to his lips. "We need to save Louis, one way or another. He deserves to be saved. We can't turn our backs on him now."

Worry was written across every line of Tyson's face, but he didn't argue with his mate; he just kissed her, and the emotions between them were strong enough that it was a tangible thing. "I love you," she murmured against his lips, and then they pulled apart.

Tyson's eyes never left the face of his redheaded witch. He watched her as she opened a step-through to Faerie. He watched her usher the other princesses through. He almost followed, but somehow managed to stop himself.

"Wait," Jacob called out just before Justice was about to disappear. She spun around, her expression blank even though there was definitely something simmering in her eyes. "Be careful," the fey Compass said. "Faerie might be the land of your birth, but it's filled with many dangers. You seem to have a natural predisposition toward trouble, and ... we might need your help back here. So ... don't die."

Justice blinked, some of the blankness fading out as stronger emotions took over. "Thank you for that heart-warming concern," she drawled. "I'm just filled with all the softer feelings."

She then turned to step through the doorway again, but spun around at the last minute and flipped him off.

When she disappeared, I noticed Jacob had the slightest smile tipping up the corner of his lips. Having met the other females in his pack, I knew the Compasses were not afraid of strong women. If anything, they seemed to embrace the strongest of supes. Justice might not realize it, but she'd just intrigued him even more with her attitude.

The doorway disappeared, and I could feel new tension in Tyson. Grace hadn't even been gone a minute and he was not doing so well.

The four Compasses and Jessa and Mischa gathered closer to me.

"Tell us what we need to do." Jessa was all business, her eyes locked on me like a laser. "I refuse to let Louis turn into something evil. There must be a way to bring him back."

I racked my brain trying to figure out what I knew that might help. "First we need to consult with the chiefs and elders. If anyone has the knowledge of how to bring him back, it will be one of them."

To my knowledge, any mages in the past who went really dark ended up dead in a battle. Most of those mages were weaker to start with, which was why they turned to the darkness, looking for power. Most of them also pushed it one step further and ended up demon touched. I wasn't sure there were any cases like Louis's. It was unique, just like the sorcerer himself.

"We can send a mass message to the other leaders," Maximus said. "We're all linked into the same global network."

I thought on this for a moment. "Can you word it so

they don't all immediately storm into Stratford guns blazing to take Louis down?"

If word reached anyone that he had gone dark, there would be panic. He was already feared. Dark Louis was their worst nightmare.

"We'll be circumspect," Braxton promised. "Unless there's no other option."

I could hear the warning in his words. If we didn't figure out how to contain Louis, they would not hesitate in taking him down.

Jessa glared at her mate. "I know you're going to try *very* hard to save Louis before you try to kill him. Or we're going to have some serious problems."

Braxton chuckled and leaned over to kiss her forehead. "Jessa babe, you know I consider Louis pack. I don't give up on pack. Not ever. We will save him, but it doesn't hurt to have a backup plan."

His eyes met mine over her head and I could see the worry bleeding through them in streaks of yellow. I nodded to show I understood. Louis was not a sorcerer to underestimate. To do so could mean death, and while we'd do everything to save him, we couldn't risk innocent lives.

"We need to check on our babies," Mischa said quietly. "If Louis is not actively destroying the town right now, I think we should take a minute to do that, and then we can meet at the town hall to reassess."

I waved my hands and nodded. "Yes, please. Go and check on those beautiful babies. I will track Louis and keep an eye on him. I'll send a message to one of you if anything happens."

The six of them all looked uneasy, and I wasn't

surprised when Jacob informed me that he'd go with me and watch my back.

Jessa gave me a quick hug just before she was about to race off. "Thank you for helping us," she murmured close to my ear. "Thank you for caring about Louis and ... not just giving up on him."

I squeezed her back for a brief moment, enjoying the hug. You could forget the simple joy in being part of the supernatural community when you'd been gone from it for so long. Supes were very tactile. They loved big and fought hard.

I wanted it back. I hadn't even realized, until I'd spent time back in the community, how much I'd missed it. We just had to finish the job of saving Louis first.

When Jessa and the others were gone, Jacob's knowing green eyes met mine. "Been a while since you've been around supes," he said quietly. "Your essence is shining right now in a way it hasn't since I first saw you."

Fae could sense energies. It used to bother me, but now I was past caring about their knowledge of my inner energy.

"I was keeping myself isolated as a form of punishment," I admitted, still raw from my own realizations a moment ago. "I've been living in Alaska for decades. In the wilderness. Just three rowdy shifters there every now and then to keep me from going completely crazy." And the occasional night in town with the humans. "I forgot..." I whispered the last part. "I have forgotten how to live and love and be a supe."

I sniffled, forcing the emotions down. A large part of me was relieved to know I could let that all go soon.

I could feel again.

I could love again.

There was just one more obstacle before I took a new path.

"Come on," I said, shaking my head. "Let's go keep an eye on Louis before he decides to level this town."

Jacob nodded in his calm way. "I have faith in Louis," he said as we started to walk. "He'll find his way back from the darkness. He's too strong not to."

His words lingered in the crisp air—it was growing colder again—like a promise. And I prayed it was true. Louis had overcome many battles in his life, but this was going to be one of the biggest. My faith was not as unwavering as Jacob's, but I wasn't giving up either. Somehow I had to find a way to repair the light in his soul, to squash the darkness back to where it always used to be. Controlled and suppressed.

I had to figure out how to bring him back to me ... so I could finally let him go.

Jacob led us to Louis's home, and as we walked I tracked dark Louis's unmoving energy, wondering what he was doing. This had been the first place he went upon returning, so there was definitely a reason.

Once we got out of the main town, we entered the sort of gardens that I'd always dreamed of living in. Louis had built his home in a stunning spot that was less like the forests of Stratford and more like a tropical wonderland. Lots of greenery, lots of wildflowers, and a picturesque waterfall that made me want to strip off my dirty clothes and dive right in to wash the sweat and grime from my body. Being in the land between definitely took a toll on your physical and mental self.

"He's still here?" Jacob murmured.

"Yes," I replied, just as quietly. "He's inside the building."

We lay low near some bushes. I was actively blocking our energy so Louis wouldn't feel our presence. I had learned a trick to this sort of magic long ago, because simply blocking us completely didn't work. It left a magical dead spot that was almost as obvious as having my energy blazing. It was much stealthier to mimic nearby animals, filtering their energy around my own—I only took enough to mask our presence and not to hurt them.

I was always the winner at hide-and-seek in Alaska.

"He's moving," I said with some urgency a few minutes later.

I waited for him to appear, trying to prepare myself for seeing him in the flesh. It had hurt to see him in soul form, but there would be ten times the impact with his soul and vessel back together. He didn't appear though; his energy just faded out of the house and then it was in the center of town.

"He's gone to the main hall," I said, scrambling to my feet. "Freaking sneaky bastard."

Jacob chuckled, and I turned to him. "Never really heard you curse. Have to say, I kind of like it. It makes you a little more approachable."

I couldn't help but laugh in return. "I actually have the worst potty mouth. See, I was raised in a time where ladies did not curse." I made my voice all gentle before grimacing. "I countered that by acting as unladylike as possible, because why the heck did I have different rules than the men? Plus, the only friends I've had in the past thirty years pretty much only know four-letter words."

Jacob laughed loudly. "Me too," he said, a few more low chuckles emerging. "Jessa's first word was fuck, and her second was you."

I shook my head, amusement cutting through me. "That doesn't surprise me at all."

It took us a few minutes to hurry through the town, and while I was stressed about what Louis was up to, I still took the time to really see the simple but architecturally intriguing buildings and small city center. I understood now why Louis had decided to settle here.

There was magic here. Energy that was almost intoxicating.

It felt like home. Something I had not truly experienced for a very long time.

Shouting broke through the tranquility then, and whatever peace I had was stolen away as I started to run. "Did you send word to the others?" Jacob asked as we full-on sprinted.

I nodded. "Yep, I let them know what's happening and that we were on our way."

Jacob's face was tense. "Let's just hope we make it in time."

Power swelled across the town, and even Jacob flinched. Both of us picked up speed, and I knew he was holding himself back to keep pace with me. "Hang on," I said, before I opened a step-through right in front of us. On the other side we emerged right at the fountain before the town hall.

To find absolute chaos.

# 8

## LOUIS

*I* felt her energy the moment she arrived in Stratford. The new power I'd embraced was giving me heightened senses. I was finding that whatever magic I used was stronger, whatever path I set out on was clearer, and if I knew a magic user very well, their power was like a beacon that I could tap into at any point.

Tyson was there as well, his magic swirling so strongly inside him that I was almost impressed. His energy was raw and reminiscent of the original gold from Faerie. The original magic I had spent so much of my time studying. The moment I was finished bringing the American supernaturals under control, I would be visiting my old friends in Faerie. It was time for them to release the power that lay there, unused.

When I was finished at my house, the ancient book I'd kept locked away firmly in my grasp, I strode out the front door, ready to head to the town hall. That's when Elizabeth's power smashed into me. Despite the fact she was using her old trick of mimicking animals nearby, I would be able to pick her out anywhere. She appeared to be alone, or at least she was managing to hide her companions. But she could never hide herself from me. I knew her. I knew every inch of her power. I'd trained her to be the sorceress she was.

Hiding from me was a waste of her time and power. She should be embracing the strength that lay deep inside of her. From a young age, she'd had a very slight fascination with the darker energy that was part of all magic, but I'd convinced her that she was powerful enough without delving into that side of magic. I'd been young and naïve myself.

Maybe it was time to talk her back into it.

Knowing she would follow, I decided to just take a step-through right to the town hall. Truth be told, I barely even needed a step-through now. I could visualize where I wanted to be, and in the next instant I was there.

The moment I appeared on the front steps, supernaturals scattered around me, which was definitely the reception I was hoping for. The reception I expected. Fear kept them under control, made them obey without thought.

Fear controlled them.

I controlled them.

"Inside," I ordered, my voice low. Power followed each word, as it always did when I spoke, but this time I let that power snap out. It would have physically hurt some of the weaker around us, but that was not my problem.

I strode into the darker room, not at all worried that I would be disobeyed. I could crush all of them with a simple snap of my finger, and they knew it. There was no way they would risk my wrath.

"Louis!" A familiar troll came into view. "What's going on? The supes are very frightened by your behavior."

I paused, my eyes dropping to the demi-fey before me. Jerak was the leader of the demi-fey; he sat on the council and held the power of his people. But to my eyes he was nothing more than the final dying embers of a flame. Frail, the fire of his energy flickering with just enough life to produce a mild warmth.

"There are going to be some changes in Stratford," I told him. "It's been growing weaker. All supernaturals have been growing weaker. I think it's time that we showed the world what we're capable of, and to make that happen, we need to strengthen our powers."

My people were done with hiding.

Jerak tilted his head to the side, the woodiness of his features extra-defined. "What has happened to you?" He breathed in and out noticeably, his eyes wide and glassy. "You're not Louis—what have you done with Louis?"

I laughed, and silence descended over the room. I took in all of the frightened faces, and I was pleased. "I'm the same Louis you've always known, but now I have the power to bring us into a new era. I have embraced all of my sorcery. I *am* the strongest mage in the world. And you all better sit the fuck down so I can explain what's about to happen."

I dismissed Jerak, walking right past him to take my rightful place on the dais. Every seat was quickly filled, and I was pleased that no one had thought to disobey me. Except, of course, my pack—none of their familiar faces were here. No doubt they were off somewhere trying to figure out how to deal with me. They didn't stand a chance, but it amused me to let them think they had one. Just for a short time.

Focusing on the crowd, I let my gaze rest heavily on them. With nothing more than a thought, the book of power, which I'd been the keeper of for most of my hundred-plus years, appeared in my hands. I'd had it hidden so that it could be revealed at the right moment. Gasps and screams rang out, and I knew the book's reputation was solidly intact. No one had forgotten the destruction it had wrought the last time it was in someone's hands. Someone who was a little dark like me.

Unlike those idiots, I would not waste pure power on something as fucking stupid as making myself rich or famous, or trying to free all the criminals from the prisons to form a gang of murderers and thieves. Both of those attempts failed, and it was at that point I hid the book away, and it had not been seen since.

Until now.

Today I was going to use it to change the supernatural world.

Turning my attention back to the crowd, I projected my voice. "You all cower before me. It pains me to see strong, powerful supernaturals act like prey. We are not prey. We will not tremble in the shadows any longer. I'm going to change our situation so that no longer do we have to deny our true selves."

No one said anything, the silence almost deafening when I trailed off. Somewhere deep inside, there was a flicker of unease, but I wasn't ready to examine the reason for that.

"I'm going to propose something," I continued conversationally, starting to walk back and forth across the stage, letting the book magically trail along beside me. "What if supernaturals stepped out of hiding? We're superior to humans in so many ways—all ways, really—and yet we are herded into small communities like animals. Forced to hide. Forced to protect our borders so that we don't face the Neanderthal-like minds of humans who want to kill anything they don't understand ... anything they *fear*." I laughed, the low thrum vibrating with power.

"We're so far superior to humans. They're basically ants, running around in their controlled environments, working for their few leaders, and living limited, finite lives. We should be controlling them, not the other way around."

Judging by the expressions facing me, it was clear my proposal was not taking everyone by surprise. Some of the fear had left their faces, and they looked ... intrigued.

Elizabeth's power slapped against me then, and it left a small ache in my chest. She was outside, and I had a feeling she'd been out there longer than I'd thought. Somehow I'd missed her arrival, but she was now moving rapidly toward me. Lucky for her, she was going to catch the end of my show.

Spinning around, I parted my hands, laying the palms flat. The book stilled its movement, and the pages flipped open. "I hold here an original book of magic," I murmured. The audience started to whisper amongst themselves, and I let them have a second before I raised my voice. "With it, I have the power of all original fey magic. When we reveal ourselves to the humans, I can take their very limited energy and I can use it to control them. We can turn them into mindless drones to be used for our bidding. When we control them all, supernaturals will become the apex predators that we should always have been. We will have all the power."

"No!" The slamming of the doors and Elizabeth's shout drew everyone's attention. They swung around to where she stood, her arms shaking as she held them out before her, her chest heaving as she fought for breath. "You can't do this, Louis."

My name trembled on her tongue before she released it, like she almost couldn't bring herself to speak the word. This had the darkness rising, anger sending it spiraling through my body again. Magic users around the room gasped as they felt my power, and I wasn't surprised to see that actual darkness swirled around my physical body. It was growing stronger, unable to be contained in the vessel.

"You are either with or against me, *Elizabeth*." She flinched when I said her name, and I briefly wondered if it was because I never used to call her by her first name. It was "Tee" mostly. It had started as a joke, because for a short time in her teen years she'd hated Elizabeth and wished her name was Teresa, but then it turned into something just between us, something that demonstrated how close we were. Best friends.

No more, though. I had no room in my life for a weakness like friends.

"Louis, you're talking about enslaving billions of humans." She took a step down the center aisle. "Turning them into nothing more than slaves. That's evil. It's not something you should even consider. We're not superior to humans, we're just different. And we've learned how to happily coexist with them. I've been living in the human world for years. So have a lot of other supernaturals. We're just like them, only with a few extra skills."

I blinked at her, trying to figure out when she'd grown so weak and pathetic. "Time in the human world has changed you," I bit out, my hands clenching at my sides. "You're perfect on the outside, but your insides are weak."

She tilted her flawless face back, the sunlight streaming across hair that was spun from gold and other metals. Elizabeth was without a doubt unsurpassed in beauty, but her weakness made her less ... appealing to me.

"I'd rather be weak than dark," she said simply, no anger in her voice. "You need to pull the darkness back, please." Her eyes looked shiny. "Please don't make me kill you."

Heat in my chest grew, and I chuckled without humor. "You think you can kill me?"

Before she could answer, I slammed the doors behind her shut, I also turned all the lights off in the large room, plunging us into darkness. I was on Elizabeth in a heartbeat, my arms closing around her tiny body as I hauled her up against me. I expected her to fight me; I was ready for the attack. Instead, she wrapped her arms and legs around me, pressing herself even closer.

That gave me a moment's pause as I tried to figure out what was happening. What sort of attack this was? "It's not an attack," she whispered, somehow sensing those thoughts. "I'm hugging you."

My breathing grew ragged. I tried to think around the heat of her body pressed so intimately against mine. For the first time a sliver of clarity returned to me, the darkness inside parting like a curtain. It started to peel back piece by piece as I ran a hand through the long, silky strands of her hair, my heart pounding against her while my dick went rock hard pressing into her center.

The light that had been absent from my life started to bloom within me. And a lot of it originated from Elizabeth. She was bright, filled with warmth and love and kindness.

*No!* I growled in my head, sucking the darkness back inside, filling up the weakness with power again. I flung her back, off me. She was taken by surprise, slamming against a nearby wall. I felt a brief pang deep inside, but I was not going to delve into that part of myself. I could not be weak ever again.

Supernaturals would not be weak any longer.

## 9

# ELIZABETH TERESA MONTGOMERY II

*J* used magic to cushion the blow, not that Louis had actually thrown me with the sort of force he could have. If I'd hit the wall, it would have only knocked the air from me, not broken bones. Still ... the fact he could do that at all told me how far he'd let the darkness in.

For a moment there, though, a very brief moment, it almost felt like I was getting through to him. When he'd grabbed me and I wrapped myself around him, holding on as tightly as I could, I'd felt him soften.

But he was a strong asshole, and he managed to fight the light.

There was a banging on the other side of the door. I figured Jacob had rounded up his brothers and they were trying to get in. I'd gone on ahead, hoping to stop whatever mass murder was taking place. The screams before had been enough for me to assume murder, but apparently it had simply been the fact that Louis was flashing around one of the most powerful and dangerous magical tomes known to supes.

Which was understandable, because there was almost no limit to what he could do using those ancient spells.

All the lights in the room flared to life again, and the sudden brightness forced my eyes closed for a moment. Louis was back on the dais now, the book open again, and he appeared to be reading. Sucking in a deep breath, I swung around and reached out for the magically sealed door.

"Come on," I growled, trying to get it open. I used multiple different magical spells, but Louis had it sealed tight. Finally, deciding subtlety wasn't working, I just placed both hands against it and blasted the hinges. With a loud crack, it split enough that Braxton could smash his way through.

Louis lifted his head, a casual and unconcerned expression on his face. "About time you made it to the party," he said, waving a hand magnanimously. I had to swallow hard when a smile lit up his face. If it wasn't for the dark glint in his eyes, and the actual darkness misting around his body, that smile was almost like the old Louis.

My body clenched as I recalled the moment he had pressed his hard length so intimately against me. It had been too long since I had been satisfied by a man, and Louis was absolutely the most attractive specimen of male.

Except for the whole "king of darkness" thing he had going on.

"Louis, what the fuck are you doing, dude?" Jessa said as she tried to storm down the aisle. A dragon shifter kept blocking her way though. "You don't get to come in here and start controlling the town. That's a solid fuck no."

Louis chuckled. "I've missed you, Jess. And since I owe you all for freeing me from the land between"—gasps from the crowd again. Thousands of supes were squished in here, and it seemed that most of them were both scared and entertained by what was going on—"I won't reprimand you for choosing to speak to me with a little less respect than I deserve."

Jessa laughed, her hands flying to her hips. "I'm giving you the exact amount of respect you deserve. While you're acting like Larky and Kristoff, evil as fuck darkness dickheads, you'll be getting exactly *zero* respect from me."

Louis's smile faded, and I knew he was drawing on his power. Braxton stepped in front of Jessa then, or at least tried to while she continued to edge him out of the way. "Don't do this, Louis," the dragon shifter said, his voice guttural. "We owe you a lot. I do not want to have to fight you. We should be on the same side, brother."

The word "brother" had a flicker of something in Louis's eyes. I could see that it affected him more than he'd probably like to admit. Just like when I thought I was reaching him, there was a moment Braxton almost got him too.

But then that moment ended.

Louis flicked out his wrist, a spell flying from one hand while the book zoomed into the other. Braxton shifted, almost changing completely into a dragon, knocking the chairs over in the immediate vicinity. Whatever Louis had sent toward them, I knew it wasn't a deadly spell. It bounced harmlessly off the toughened skin of the partially shifted dragon.

It had only been a distraction. Louis needed us to look away long enough for him to find his spell and start reciting it without interruption.

"No!" I screamed, because I recognized the ancient words leaving his lips. I knew right then exactly what Louis was planning on doing, and it could destroy the world we had built. It could destroy the entire supernatural community.

The Compasses and Lebrons swung in my direction, and only Mischa looked terrified, but I could see the worry hidden deep inside the others. Most of them were not magic users, and there was only so much they could do to combat a spell. Especially one coming from a sorcerer of Louis's level.

"Magic users," I shouted again, projecting my voice. "On your feet now." I was going to need their energy if I wanted a hope in hell of stopping Louis. "NOW!"

Chairs scraped as supes pushed their way to standing, moving toward the center of the room. "What's happening, Lizzie?" Jessa asked. "What's he doing?"

Louis waved his hand then and tried to halt those moving, but I had expected that and my counterspell hit him in the chest, knocking him back a few feet. Bastard didn't lose his grip on the book though, and he never faltered as he continued to weave his magic—his eyes locked tightly on me, the purple turning into something molten.

"Lizzie!" Jessa said again with more force.

Pulling my gaze from Louis, I focused on her for a second, because that was all the time I had to spare. "He's exposing us to the humans. This spell is going to broadcast supernaturals to the world. Our locations. The prisons. Our powers and abilities. He is going to expose us in a way that means we would never be able to hide in the human world again. And if they react badly—"

"Which they always do," Maximus bit out.

I nodded. "Yes, then we'll be at war."

Again. I was so fucking done with war.

"Why is he doing this?" a magic user nearby asked. Her eyes were very green against her dark skin, her face perfect and angular like a model's.

"Because he wants to control them," I guessed, having missed a lot of his speech. "He wants to have all the power and all of the control. He probably believes that it makes us weak to hide like we do."

Which was partly true. One on one, even the weakest supe could take down a human, no worries. But en masse, humans were easily panicked and dangerous.

"He did say something about control," another magic user said. "About an army of slaves."

Louis was not in his right mind; the darkness liked power and would constantly strive for more. We had to stop him. "I'm going to need to contain Louis," I told them all. "Stop him before he finishes the spell."

A spell as big as he was weaving was going to take a lot of time to complete, but we still had to hurry. I heard the murmurs and agreement from those around me, and I started to weave my own magic. "Connect to the ley line," I told them all.

Through the line, I could utilize their magic as well as my own. Of course, Louis was probably connected to the line as well, so we had to be careful that we didn't give him access to our powers. The last thing he needed was more of a boost.

"Guess we're getting a front-row seat to an important lesson in dark magic," someone muttered nearby. I didn't deny it. This was the reason magic users had it hammered so hard into them: do not mess with demons or dark magic, because it didn't end well for anyone.

I couldn't focus on that. I had to concentrate on my spell. I had to stop Louis before he changed the fundamentals of our world.

The line thrummed strongly beneath my feet; Stratford had one of the strongest in America. I felt the presence of the hundreds of supes with me, all of our energies mingling together. Louis's power was further away, and I had a sudden thought that maybe we could fight him in the actual ley lines. He would not be able to power this spell without it, so if I could eject him and block him for a short period, we might be able to detain him.

My center burned then as the light of my magic started to rise from my body. Louis was probably more powerful than he'd ever been, because dark magic seemed to have no limit, but there was a universal truth: light always beat the dark. That's why almost all magic users were able to contain the darker side of their power, because light triumphed. It was only in rare circumstances, like Louis's, when something diminished the light so much that it couldn't burn bright enough, that the darkness won.

I just had to figure out how to reignite that illumination inside Louis.

Gathering as much energy as I could from those around me, I sent a powerful force along the line toward

Louis, hoping to take him by surprise. We failed spectacularly at that, and instead of blasting him out, we ended up receiving a pulse back that was so strong it made my teeth ache.

I dug deeper and tried something different, whispering a simple spell to freeze his power, locking him into one section of ley line. That would stop him from having access to most of the energy here, and for a split second he'd be frozen in his physical form.

Then I could put the second part of my plan into action.

Taking more power from those around me, I repeated my spell, and this time it went exactly to plan. He'd clearly been expecting a different sort of attack, something more aggressive than my simple little spell. Reinforcing the box that was holding him immobile, I brought most of my focus out of the ley line and started to run.

Louis's body was frozen, but already I could see his eyes moving as he broke free from my power. How in the hell was he strong enough to take on hundreds of magic users? It was impossible, and yet he continued to do the impossible. Over and over. His mouth opened, and I knew a spell was about to emerge, but I was on the dais now, moving into him. I shot the book away with magic before launching myself at him.

My power wrapped around us both as I bound his body to mine, keeping his magic immobilized in the only way I knew how. He was too strong for me to take down one-on-one, but in this moment of weakness I could bind his energy and tie it to mine so he wouldn't be able to do any magic without my agreement. I wouldn't be able to do any without his either, but that was a risk I was willing to take until I could turn him back to the light.

With a final click, the spell locked us into place, and I slowly released him, backing away. His eyes resembled amethysts, the purple almost crystalline as they glittered at me.

"You're going to regret that," he said, his low voice bringing goose bumps to my skin. "Especially because you're too late."

"What do you mean?" I whispered.

He smiled, which turned his face into a flawless work of art. "The spell was complete. You were too late, Elizabeth. Just like always."

The room erupted then, shouts and crying filling the air.

"Take it back," I said, my focus locked on Louis. "You can reverse it now before the damage is done. Before you condemn us all to a war with the humans. You know better than almost anyone here"—except for me—"that war means our people will die. You cannot let that happen."

He shrugged. "I don't think they will. And if they do, it will only be the weak, and that isn't necessarily a bad thing. We should step into this new era the strongest we can be. So ... it's a sacrifice that I believe is best for the majority."

I blinked at him. "Do you even hear the words that are coming out of your mouth? How can you say something like that? How can you talk so casually about ending lives? Who the hell are you?"

He opened his mouth again, but an eerie whistle drew his attention. I turned as well, my blood going cold when I realized it was the whooshing of wings as dragons filled the area just outside the building. Through the open doors, I could see them. And it looked like there were dozens of them. Wild dragons. I felt their energy, and as the huge gold beast in the center pushed her massive head through the door, I knew this was Jessa's dragon: Josephina.

Her energy vibrated through the hall, and I heard a low grunt then as Maximus dropped to his knees. "Everyone out of the way," Braxton growled. "He's going to shift. He can't control the first shift."

The wild dragons had brought Maximus's dragon. The mating bond was complete.

Supes scattered as the Compasses hauled their brother outside. I heard more shouts, and then there was the distinct sound of bones breaking before a dragon roar filled the air. I caught only a glimpse of Maximus's beast as it flew past, the scales a deep, rich brown color, like newly turned dirt.

Tilting my head back, I was surprised to find Louis casually leaning against a nearby pillar, amusement spiking across his face. "I don't think the dragons are here for me," I told him, spitting the words because I was so angry. "You should be a little more worried."

He shrugged, those broad shoulders shifting under his robes. "They're only making my job that much easier. Right now, the supernatural world is being broadcast into the human world. Our energy will draw them in now instead of repelling them, and it's only a matter of time before they show up on our doorstep. Having the dragons here will make it that much easier for me to instill fear and respect in those ants."

"You think the humans will submit to us?" I asked. "That if you expose the darker side, the prisons, the dragons and vampires, that humans will freak out and beg for protection...?"

Louis straightened; he towered over me, and I had to swallow hard. He was so much of everything. And it was very disconcerting.

"I would prefer that the humans feared us," he admitted slowly. "It would make the transition easier."

My right hand trembled as I forced myself not to touch him. I couldn't understand why I wanted to so badly, but there was something in Louis that had always called to me. "Why did you let her die?" he asked me then, and his subject change knocked the breath from me. "You knew someone was stalking her, and you never even told me."

This wasn't technically true. Regina had admitted that she was having an issue with a local witch, Taylor. This witch had envied my sister's power, and most importantly, she had envied her having Louis. But Regina had asked me not to say anything. She wasn't worried.

"She thought she could deal with it herself," I said, sadness in my tone. "Neither of us realized how psycho Taylor actually was. If I had thought for one second that she was planning on hurting Reggie..."

Louis flinched as I used her nickname, his huge body tense as he sucked in a long breath. "I've blamed you for her death for a long time," he told me. "But now I see that it was Regina's fault. She was cocky and she didn't trust me with her problems. My power has given me clarity, and I'm ready to move past the grief that immobilized me for so many years."

Talking to him like this, he almost felt like the old Louis. If it wasn't for the darkness swirling around his body, I wouldn't have been able to tell at all. "You need to stop this spell," I said again, this time taking a step closer. "There's other ways to slowly bring us into the human world, ways that would not create mass hysteria. I think you should consider that maybe you've jumped in too hard and fast, and we should dial it back a little."

"This is the best way—" he started to say, but was cut off as powerful sorcerers filled the room. My eyes landed on Braxton and Jessa, both of whom were back in the hall, watching Louis and me closely.

"Elders," Louis spat. "One more thing I have to deal with."

Apparently the Compasses hadn't quite been circumspect enough when they'd searched for answers, or word had gotten out some other way. There were hundreds of terrified supes here, and any one of them might have called for help.

Louis stepped forward, lifting his hands to cast magic at them. He must have forgotten that I had bound our powers, though. I felt the swell of energy as he reached for the ley line, and the tap on my power as well as it sought for me to release it and allow him access.

I refused, locking my energy down and reinforcing the block.

"Release me!" Louis growled.

I shook my head. "No!"

"Louis!" roared an older sorcerer. He was grizzled, nearing the end of his long life, but he was definitely powerful. "You need to stop this spell now. Already there are humans at the edge of Stratford."

Louis ignored him, his focus on me. "Lizzie, I will not ask you again. Release my magic."

I hated when he called me Lizzie. I hated when he called me Elizabeth. And the bastard knew that.

"You're going to have to kill me," I said slowly.

He moved toward me until he crowded right over me, using his size to intimidate me. If I hadn't been short for my entire life, it might even have worked. But I was used to being the smallest, and it didn't bother me anymore.

"You're a part of my past that I would be happy to never revisit again," he growled down at me, "but I don't want to kill you."

The unspoken "I will if I have to, though" remained between us.

"We will give you to the count of five, Louis, and then we attack."

That threat was from more than one sorcerer; the room was slowly filling as more reinforcements entered.

I noticed Jessa had wiggled her way out from under Braxton; she was near the stage gesturing to me. "Lizzie, get out of there," she hissed. "Psycho Louis is not to be trusted."

It was true, but I couldn't bring myself to move just yet.

"Five! ... Four! ... Three!"

Louis didn't look worried. "You better release my power or we're both about to die," he said causally, sounding more relaxed than I'd heard him in a long time.

In that moment, I briefly considered releasing him, because survival instinct is always strongest when you're closest to death. But I knew there was no way I could allow him to kill all of these sorcerers. Our elders and chiefs were too important. Their knowledge could not be lost yet.

I would protect them.

"Two! ... Last chance, Louis." Brief pause. "One!"

"Louis!" Jessa screamed as the final number rang out.

Power blasted in a single concentrated burst, heading straight for Louis. His eyes locked with mine. My breath caught, throat already burning with unshed tears, and I had no idea why I did it, but my legs were moving before my brain even caught up.

I threw myself in front of Louis, taking the full force of the killing blow. It hit me in the chest, burning through me. The pain was so intense that I was screaming before I fully registered what had happened. The force knocked me back into Louis, and as his arms wrapped around me, my dying soul reached out for anything to save it, to keep it here in this world.

It sounded like thunder in my ears as our souls smashed together, his dark and mine light, but in that moment they bonded in a way that only true mates could.

*Louis is my true mate?* I had that moment of knowledge before the pain became too much and my heartbeat stuttered a few more times, then everything went dark.

## 10

# LOUIS

The moment Elizabeth locked our powers together, giving her the ability to control my spells, the darkness started pushing me to destroy her, to destroy the person who thought they could control us.

I couldn't bring myself to do it, though. She was just too perfect and powerful, and I might need her at some point. That was the only reason. Nothing else.

When the sorcerers arrived, I expected her to release her control. These mages did not mess around, and she knew she could be killed in the crossfire. But the stubborn sorceress just locked her power down, and mine, and refused to budge.

They started to count, and I watched Elizabeth. Her bravery intrigued me; why the hell had I always been so fascinated by this woman? No matter what I did, I couldn't shake her from my life. From my mind.

She kept looking between the elders and me, her brow so furrowed that it was almost comical. I braced myself when they reached their final countdown, knowing I would have to try and counter their spell somehow. One last time I urged Elizabeth to release us, but she refused. Going down with the ship apparently. Always so noble.

The spell blasted at me with force. I wondered if I would be strong enough to take it. I had time to move, because I was anticipating it, but before I could make the decision about which way to go, Elizabeth shocked the hell out of me. A roar left me as she jumped and intercepted the spell that was meant for me.

In slow motion, I reached for her, but it was too late. The blast hit her in the chest, knocking her back into me. She felt so small as I cradled her, keeping us both from hitting the ground. Her screams filled my ears, and my heart beat at a frantic pace. That had been a blow designed to take down a powerful sorcerer, and while Elizabeth was strong, she was not quite at my level.

As I was pulling her tighter, trying to spin her around so I could assess the damage, I felt a thud in my chest that was followed by the sort of warmth I had never experienced before. Warmth and light split through the darkness that had been part of me since the demon world.

*A true mate bond?*

Tee was my true mate.

My oldest friend in the world, someone I had cut out of my life in grief and fear and pain... She was my mate, and her light had chased the darkness from my soul. Hers was the only light that could, because it shone so brightly.

I mentally reached for her, feeling her life slipping away through our newly formed bond.

Her screams died off; her head lolled to the side, and

her heartbeat, under my hand, started to slow, each beat getting more erratic as life left her body.

"No!" I roared, power shooting from me in long waves. That's when I knew this was bad, because only death, or near death, could have broken the spell she'd placed on us.

"Tee," I said hoarsely, my hands sliding up from where they rested against the ragged laceration in her chest. An urge to smash those magic users into dust came over me, and if the darkness had still held me in its grip, I would not have hesitated. But Tee had given me the strength to come back to the light.

And I knew the truth. This was not the magic users' fault.

It was mine.

Again, I was about to be the cause of my mate's death.

"Tee, please, I need you to hold on for me while I heal you," I whispered as I lowered her to the ground, all of her glorious hair spilling across us.

My hands went to her chest and I tried desperately to calm my frazzled nerves as I filled her with healing energy. If she hadn't been so powerful—and the newly formed bond with me was helping as well—she'd already be dead.

I poured everything I had into the healing, because despite all of the history between us, Elizabeth had always been important to me. And she had sacrificed herself to save me.

*True mate.*

If I lost a second mate, I would not be in this world any longer. I could not do it. My emotions already ran so deeply, and my need to bring her back to me was stronger than anything I'd ever felt before. A sliver of darkness tried to rise from the depths I'd locked it in, teasing me with its power, power that might be able to save my mate, but I did not consider it for a second. She'd brought me back to the light, had fought for me and saved my life. I would not let her down by embracing the darkness again.

I would not touch darkness ever again.

*But what if she dies?*

That thought stole my breath, and I poured more healing into her. Thankfully, her wound sealed, and the last of the attacking spell left her body. A sigh of relief rushed from me when her heartbeat picked up, resuming a normal pace. Once I was done healing her as best as I could, I gathered her into my arms, only noticing then that I was surrounded on all sides. Strong emotions, which had been dulled by the darkness, swelled within me when I saw Jessa close by.

"Jess," I said softly. "I'm so sorry."

She shook her head, her eyes filling with tears as she swallowed hard. "No," she choked out. "It's not your fault. This is because you went to the demon land. You did that for us, and you suffered so much because of it."

She launched herself at me then, and Braxton didn't even try and stop her. "I'm so glad you're back," she cried into my chest. I managed to hold her and Tee, both women so very precious to me.

"She's okay, right?" Jessa said as she pulled back slightly. Her eyes locked on Tee's face, which was right by hers.

I nodded, watching Tee closely, happy to see color back in her cheeks. "I healed most of the damage, and now her body is in a recuperative sleep. She will probably be unconscious for a few days."

A throat cleared nearby, and I met the ancient eyes of Rufus, a sorcerer who I'd had a very good relationship with. Well, until today.

"You came back from the darkness," he said slowly, eyeing me with some suspicion.

"Tee … Elizabeth is my true mate," I told him truthfully. "Our souls bonded … in her dying moments. That was the catalyst we needed. Her light chased away the darkness."

More of the tension in the crowd around me faded, and I gently dropped Jessa to her feet. Tee remained cradled in my arms. "I know that you're all going to want an explanation from me," I said, looking between the familiar faces. "And I plan on doing everything I can to rectify the situation I have created here, but right now I need to ensure my mate continues to heal. She keeps the darkness at bay for me, and if she dies…." I trailed off, because everyone already knew what would happen. They knew that Tee was the only thing stopping me from destroying the world. If the darkness came back, I would be a mindless monster. Much worse than before. I would take the world down with me, and there was nothing anyone could do to stop me.

The fragile supe in my arms was the only thing stopping the world from ending.

## 11

# ELIZABETH TERESA MONTGOMERY II

*I* had regrets. So many regrets. I was not ready to die yet, not when I'd only just decided to start living, but sometimes you didn't get a say in that. Sometimes your number was up and you had no choice but to accept the inevitable.

The warmth in my body increased, and just when I felt like my time on this world was done, the pain faded. With that came energy and clarity, and I had no idea how long I had drifted in my semi-dead state, but eventually I realized I was not dying any longer.

I'd been saved.

There was only one sorcerer with that sort of power. Louis had saved me, brought me back from the twilight of death, and there was so much light and warmth in my chest that I almost felt like I was on fire.

As I rose from unconsciousness, his deep voice was the first thing I heard. "...I remember the first day I saw you. Gods, you couldn't have been more than five or six, and you had so much hair, even then. It was spread out around you, like a golden cloak, as you ran through the field. You were so wild. Wild in a way that I never saw from Regina. It was like more life filled you than the rest of us, and you embraced it. That was the day I decided we would be best friends, and you thought that was an amazing idea."

I remembered that day so clearly. Louis had been two years older than me, and I worshipped him. His family was wealthy. They lived on the good side of town and had all the respect of the supernatural community. We, on the other hand, were not wealthy, and in those days there wasn't as much money to go around our communities, so we were looked down on. Even worse, my parents were not powerful. In fact, my mother never even made it to sorceress, spending all of her days as a witch. Louis befriending me caused a lot of talk, but we didn't care. Our friendship blossomed and strengthened over the years. The first supe to ever come between us was Regina. My sister hadn't liked Louis much when we were growing up, treating him like an annoying younger brother even though they were the same age.

Until she no longer saw him that way.

I still had no idea what had made her pursue him like she did. One day she just saw him differently. It was the same for me, but I spent too long worrying about the consequences, and she beat me to it. Then he was smitten, falling hard for my charismatic sister.

My eyelids fluttered open, hazy memories washing away as I blinked. Sunlight was streaming in from the open bay windows nearby, and when I could finally see clearly, it was all greenery out there. I pulled my gaze from that view to meet a pair of purple-blue eyes. We stared for a few long moments. "Hey," he said, his voice raspy.

"Hey," I said back, my voice breaking.

Louis looked so beautiful, no darkness surrounding him, his handsome face filling my vision. I remembered very clearly that we had a bond; it was beating in my chest strongly, and my body ached to touch him, but I resisted. Just because we were true mates did not mean that we could make this work. There was so much history between us. Maybe too much. This was almost a cruel happening for us both. But I was grateful that it had brought him back to the light. Killing Louis would have killed me, and now I understood why.

We were true mates. Two halves of the same whole. Bound by fate.

When Louis leaned forward, I expected soft and kind words to come out of his mouth; instead his eyes darkened as he growled, "If you ever, and I mean *ever*, attempt to jump in front of magic meant to take me down again, I will kill you myself, Elizabeth Teresa Montgomery."

I blinked at him, not sure at what I was hearing. "W-what?"

Louis bared his teeth, and I almost flinched back. "You nearly died. If our bond hadn't kicked in, allowing light back into my magic, I would not have been in a position to save you." He was on his feet then, power flowing almost visibly around him. "You almost died!"

He was just short of yelling, and I was both fearful of and fascinated by the new Louis I saw before me. He was glorious, his gorgeous face filled with hard lines and his power washing across everything. It appeared the darkness was gone, but ... it had changed him.

I struggled to pull myself higher in the bed, still aching despite the fact I was fully healed. He let out a low curse and rushed to my side, lifting me into a sitting position with ease. "You need to rest," he reminded me, tucking some of his emotions away again.

He was watching me so closely. I found it harder to breathe when he was like this.

"Are you sure the darkness is completely gone?" I pressed. I was pretty sure, but pretty sure wasn't enough in situations like this.

Louis seemed to consider his answer for a moment. "It's gone, but part of my energy has been changed. It's almost restless now. My power has a different edge to it." His fists clenched. "But as long as you remain in this world, I will remain in the light."

I understood what he was saying about the restlessness. There was a feral sort of energy about his magic now. "So no pressure, hey?" I tried to lighten the mood. "I'll do my best not to die, because dark Louis wasn't my favorite."

He didn't smile. His face shut down and more black swirled in his eyes. "Losing control of myself will never be something I'm proud of," he admitted, lowering his gaze to the side of the bed. "And I managed to create a bit of a problem that looks to be more difficult than I expected to clean up."

I remembered then. "The spell!" I blurted. "What happened with the spell?"

His expression remained blank. "Once I knew you were fine, I reversed the spell itself, and for the most part the humans were unharmed and ended up back in their normal lives...."

"But..." I pressed, because I sensed a huge but in that statement.

"But some supes, elders, and council leaders around the world decided that my plan was a solid one."

"They exposed us to the humans?" I whispered, understanding exactly what he was saying.

Louis nodded, and his jaw clenched hard. "Yes, they finished what I started and broadcast our world on live television."

"Fuck," I breathed, and for a brief moment amusement lit up Louis's face. He'd always loved it when I cursed, because he said it was so unexpected.

"Can you reverse what they've done?" I asked, wondering what the next plan of action was.

Louis leaned back in his chair, his broad shoulders spilling over the sides as he lifted both hands. "It's out of my hands. The only way is a mass vote agreeing to let me stop this. It was a decision by the elders and chiefs, and only a worldwide vote by all leaders can reverse it."

"Shouldn't something like that have had to be agreed on by all supes in the first place?"

There were laws about this sort of thing, about exposing us to the human world.

Louis nodded. "Yes, but I broke that law when I set the initial spell in motion. I opened up the opportunity for the others, and they took it."

Louis was lucky he wasn't in prison right now. Speaking of... "How are you not in prison?"

That amusement was back. "Who could they send to put me in there?"

Right.

"There's always me," I suggested in a dry tone.

A smile spread across his face, the first true one I'd seen from him. "You're literally the only one with the power." His husky voice sent shivers down my spine, and I fought against the urge to throw myself into his arms.

*No.* No, this was not happening. Sometimes fate was not enough to overcome the past.

"Are we going to talk about it?" Louis must have been reading my facial expression, because he brought up the very thing I was thinking. "About our bond."

Swallowing roughly, I shook my head. "What's there to talk about? We're true mates, it's a shock for sure, but … we have too much history, Louis. There's no way we can just ignore all of that and fall into…." I waved my hand between us. "Fall into whatever between us."

"You don't even want to give it a shot?" His tone held curiosity, and I wished I knew what he was thinking. He seemed to be so calm, while I was a total mess inside, emotions churning through me with so much force I felt sick.

"Do you want to give it a shot?" I turned the question back on him. "You loved my sister. You mourned her for decades. You … left me. How the hell do we get past all of that?"

Annoyance crashed through me when I realized my throat was scratchy and my eyes burned. I was almost shouting. I was not allowed to cry, no godsdamn way.

Louis looked like he was going to reach for me, but at the last moment pulled back. "I didn't just mourn her," he said, glittering eyes locking me in place. "I mourned you both. You disappeared when Regina died. There was that moment in Faerie, and then I never saw you again. *You left me*, Tee. After everything we'd been through, I needed you in my life more than ever."

In some ways he did speak the truth. I'd been filled with guilt because part of me had despised my sister for what she had and I didn't. Then when she died, I'd basically lost my mind, shutting myself off from the world, angry and heartbroken. Then my isolation grew into a habit. I found it more and more difficult to leave my house. Outside of my friends in the mountains, I was basically a hermit. Part of me though, and this was a stupid part of me, had expected Louis to come and find me. Only he never had.

Before I could stop him, Louis wrapped his hands around mine, encasing them in his warmth and strength. My heart skipped a few beats, and I felt heat rise across my body as parts of me that had been dead for a long time stormed to life.

*Well, hey there, vagina. Nice of you to pop up and say hello.* I hadn't had sex for years, which for supes was more like centuries, but still ... not the best timing.

"Louis—" I started, but he cut me off.

"I'm not sure how I feel right now," he told me, "but I do know that we were brought back together for a reason. We should at least get to know each other again, see if there is anything more than just the bond between us. I don't know if I can be a mate to you ... I don't even know if I want to be a mate again and risk that sort of pain, but I also don't want you to leave."

I choked out a rough laugh. "You don't know if you

want this, but you still think we should stick around and get to know each other? As far as I can see, despite the bond, all that's going to happen is our supernatural instincts will push and push until we're wrapped so far around each other that I can't tell whose limbs are whose."

Louis's lips twitched and his eyes filled with mirth. "And that would be a bad thing?"

The ache in my chest deepened. "Yes, because it's just sex. And that's not enough for me any longer. I'm too old and broken just to be a powerful mage's plaything." He was killing me. I had loved Louis for years, and it would be so easy to just take whatever he offered. But until he knew for sure what he wanted, he would always hold me at a distance, and I had the sneaking suspicion that that would hurt more than never having him.

"You could have chosen me years ago, but you picked Regina," I reminded him.

The grip on my hands tightened minutely. "You never gave me any indication that you wanted to be more than friends," he bit out. "Not one. Back then I would have made the move the moment you did."

I yanked my hands free. "You should have made the move. Who the hell do you think you are, just waiting around for us to all declare ourselves so you could pick and choose?"

Men were so freaking dense at times; it was beyond frustrating.

We were both on our feet now. I'd slipped out of the bed and was standing there in what looked like an old shirt of Louis's. It hung to midthigh on me, leaving a lot of leg bare. His gaze traveled down the length for a brief moment before making its way back to my face.

"We were both afraid to ruin our friendship," he said, his eyes pleading with me to understand. "It wasn't about me wanting to choose between you and Regina. It was always you, until I realized that I was only ever going to be a friend to you. Then ... I got caught up in Regina. She was amazing, there's no denying it, and our relationship was good. Losing her... The guilt almost destroyed me. I can't risk that again."

My sister had been amazing. I was never surprised that Louis fell in love with her. She was tall and smart and powerful. She had long raven black hair and big blue eyes. She was so different to me that most people never even believed we were sisters. And I had loved her.

Louis took a step closer to me, his chest almost touching mine. "This is new ... a shock. We should take some time to get to know each other again. I miss my friend. I miss you, Tee."

Everything hurt in that moment: my body, my heart, and my eyes from the burning tears threatening to fall. "Friends ... is not going to work for me."

I pushed against him, my hands slamming on the hard planes of his chest. There was no way I could have moved him if he wanted to fight me, but thankfully he took a step back and gave me some breathing room. I was feeling as feral in that moment as the light in his eyes had been.

"I'm going to have a shower and get cleaned up," I said quietly, never taking my gaze off him. "Can you tell me where my clothes are?"

"I had them all brought here." He waved a hand

toward a nearby dresser. "You've been out for a few days. I wanted you close by, so you're in my home."

Of course I was.

I nodded and waited until he started to move toward the door. "Bathroom is through there," he said, pointing to another door nearby. "Call me if you need anything."

Yeah, that was a big fat *never going to happen* right there. I would literally drown before I called out for his help, especially while I was naked. But I just smiled and nodded, and then moved to open the drawers of the dresser, pulling out underwear, jeans, and a white shirt.

When I was safely locked in the bathroom, I allowed myself a minute to fall apart, turning the shower on full blast. The noise hid my small gasps as tears ran down my cheeks. I didn't cry much anymore. Strong emotions were not part of my world. But in that brief second I wasn't sure I would survive the pain in my heart.

Louis ... how could he be my true mate? How could fate be so cruel? To have separated us for all these years, only to pull us together now when we truly couldn't be mates...

*Your choice.* My inner voice reminded me that it wasn't fate's fault. She put us in each other's paths from childhood. My pain was from my own fears, and my own bad choices. Louis's as well. Both of us were to blame. We had ignored the path and suffered greatly for it.

Another sob choked out of me, and I struggled to stuff my emotions back inside. If I left the room with the evidence of my crying session across my face, I'd have to deal with Louis, and he was relentless when he was trying to get to the bottom of something. He would not stop until I poured all of my feelings out in the open.

Which was redundant, because nothing I felt could change reality.

He didn't want to risk the pain of us developing this into a true mate bond, and I didn't want to be someone's "sort of" mate just because the true bond pulled us closer. Eventually my tears dried and I got in the shower. The warm water beating down on me was soothing, and as I stood there under the hot spray I decided that I wouldn't stay in Stratford any longer. I was going to go back home, for a while at least. Louis would be busy dealing with the elders, and I needed some distance. Time apart would hopefully give us clarity, and then ... we could both reassess.

Some of the weight had lifted from my chest by the time I got out. I'd always liked a plan of action, even if I didn't always want to follow it. At least my brain was focused, and that let me not dwell on how shitty the situation was. When I was dry and dressed, I pulled my long hair up into a messy bun, letting tendrils fall around my face. The messy bun was literally the greatest creation since fey wine.

Stepping into my room, I was relieved to see the door still closed. Louis had exceptional hearing, and I'd been worried that he might have heard my tears and would be waiting for me. When I opened the door out of my room, I let out a gasp. On the other side it looked like a tornado had gone through the place. Furniture was upside down, glass was smashed everywhere, and there appeared to be enough feathers to fill a small city.

"Hey!"

My head snapped up to see a familiar supe standing amongst the chaos.

"Jessa, hey!" I said, hurrying toward her, stepping over debris. "Where did Louis go? And ... what happened in here?"

Jessa looked around, a wry grin tipping up her lips. "Louis has exceptional hearing," she said, repeating my thought from a moment ago. "And he makes things explode when a woman he cares about is crying."

I slammed my mouth closed, reaching up to rub at my tender eyes. "He heard me crying in the shower?"

She nodded. "Yeah, and he didn't take it very well. I convinced him not to smash the door down and surprise you with his fury, and Braxton has taken him out into the meadow for some cool-down time."

"He did all of this while I was in the shower?" I said, trying not to cry again. The mate bond drove supes insane at times, that was for sure.

"No."

My head snapped up and I met her blue eyes.

"He did most of this when you almost died. He brought you here, and he was not in a good place. Which for someone of Louis's power..."

"Is very dangerous," I finished, somewhat breathlessly.

All of a sudden, panic filled me. This was too much. The bond was too strong already. We would not be able to fight the pull. It was going to take all of our choices away, and I refused to let that happen. I needed to be away from him while I tried to think about the future. About what I wanted.

Lurching forward, I grabbed Jessa's hands. Her concerned expression met mine. "I need your help," I whispered. "I need to leave. Right now. I'm going back home, because Louis and I both need time to think about everything and decide what we want."

Her tanned skin paled. "Lizzie, dude, I really like you. I think we'd all have died without your help, and for that you're family to me, but ... there's nothing that can stop Louis if he wants something. I really think you should talk this over and explain to him that you're leaving."

I shook my head violently. "No. No, it won't work. The bond will stop him from letting me go. Even though he knows, deep down, that it's better if we're apart, at least while we both deal with our feelings."

Jessa didn't look convinced, but she didn't argue again either. Her head flicked to the door for a beat, before coming back to me. "Louis is occupied right now. The dragons have come to visit."

It was only then I remembered the wild dragons who had arrived when the spell was cast. "They're still here?" I asked.

Jessa nodded. "Yes, they came because it was time for Maximus to bond to his dragon soul. But it's now time for them to return."

An idea came to me. "I'm going to go with them," I told her quietly. "My transition from Faerie to Earth will take at least five Earth days. That will give Louis time to think about what he wants. Give him the space he needs to deal with this revelation."

"What about you?" Jessa asked.

I laughed without humor. "I have loved Louis since I was five. He was my best friend, the one who got me through every fucking hard moment of life. But he also broke my heart. Shattered it into a million pieces when he chose my sister as his mate."

The pain still felt like it was strangling me.

Jessa's expression was sympathetic. "I'm not going to defend Louis here, because I don't know enough about the situation, but, Lizzie, you should have seen him when you got hurt. He held you like you were precious. He looked at you like he would never see another thing outside of your face. That love you felt ... it was not one-sided. Louis was devastated when you almost died. Maybe the two of you just need to explore this bond between you. Stop fighting it."

I wrapped my arms tightly around myself to try and prevent my pain from leaking out. Like ... her words had actually cut into my skin, and I was bleeding from the agony.

"Is it ever too late?" I whispered. "Is there a point where too much has happened ... there's no way we could be together..."

She shook her head. "While you both breathe, you still have hope."

I choked on a sob, my chest aching. "I think ... I think we both need a few days. At least. This is a shock to us, and there is no way to make a decision while in shock. If Louis chooses to follow me, chooses to explore this mate bond, he'll know where I am. If I go via Faerie, he'll be forced to wait a few days, which will give him time to think."

Jessa threw her head back and laughed. "Girl, you're delusional if you think he's not going to follow you. He's going to be on your ass in all kind of ways."

Before I could stop myself, I laughed too. She had grown on me, and I was going to miss her. "I'm mostly trying to give us some time. Please let him know that."

Despite the spells that were hiding me in Alaska, I knew Louis would find me when I returned. If that's what he decided he wanted.

"They're leaving," Jessa whispered. "Louis and Brax are heading back this way. If you want to leave at the same time, you need to do it now."

Leaning forward, I hugged her tightly, and she gave me a squeeze in return. "I'll see you soon," she said, her earthy scent surrounding me. "And don't be too hard on Louis. He loves deeply, even if it takes him some time to figure out what he wants."

I just nodded, because some of what she said was true.

"Back door is that way," Jessa said, pushing me toward a large blue door near the impressive kitchen. "Josephina is waiting for you."

Jessa must have asked her to wait, and I was eternally grateful. With one more squeeze, I let go of her hand and turned, hurrying from the room. I could feel Louis's energy closing in, and with it the warm sensations in my chest increased. It was his presence ... our bond tugging us together.

My pace picked up and I practically burst out the back door. In the clearing a little ways away was a huge golden dragon. She sat still, watching me closely as I moved toward her. Her eyes were wide and ancient, filled with knowledge and wisdom so far beyond anything I'd ever seen.

*Hurry.*

The word filtered through my mind and I picked up the pace. Magic started to build around her, and I reached her side just in time for the peak of her energy.

We were then hurtling toward Faerie, and I was zooming away from Louis.

This had been my choice ... my plan ... but in that moment my heart broke a little.

This was the best thing for everyone. I had to believe that.

**12**

---

# LOUIS

he dragons surrounded me, each of them filtering thoughts to me. They were heading back to Faerie now. Maximus was handling his new bond without issue, and while they'd stayed an extra day to argue with the council members, the current situation here on Earth was not their problem. This wasn't their home.

Josephina did leave me with one warning though. *I fear that this is going to lead to war. The humans are not dealing well with this new reality, and it has only been a few days and minimal exposure. If you stand any chance of returning things to what they were, now is the time. Tomorrow might be too late.*

She was right. I already knew we were balancing on the edge of a situation I could not control. Very soon there would be too much exposure. Now was the only chance we had.

But I also had another situation I needed to deal with: my mate.

My anger and pain at hearing her cry had not faded; my energy roiled angrily inside of me, wanting a place to go. Thankfully, the darkness remained buried under the light, so I didn't have to worry about that, but I was a little concerned by how volatile my emotions already were in regards to Tee.

We needed some time together to explore this bond. I hadn't lied to her before; I still wasn't sure that I was good enough for her anymore, too old and broken from the pains of the past, but we both deserved a chance.

Tee was wrong about one thing, though. I never abandoned her. I'd known exactly where she was all of these years. I'd kept an eye on her, missing my friend. I figured when she was ready to forgive me for Regina, she would come and find me, but she never had.

We'd both wasted so much time, each of us punishing ourselves.

There was one irrefutable truth though: losing Tee again was not something I could deal with. At the moment, as long as she lived the darkness was contained. Which was what had me hesitating about deepening the bond. I was scared to lose control of myself again if I felt even more deeply than I did right now.

Would it really make any difference though? Even if she died right this minute, I would be destroyed.

I was already fighting not to go back to her.

"Come on," Braxton said when we'd been standing in the clearing for some time, letting nature soothe some of the ragged edges. "Jessa is waiting for us."

Jessa had basically kicked her mate and me out the door, saying she'd talk to Tee. Make sure she was okay after the crying. Probably a better idea than blasting the door down, which was what I'd wanted to do.

"You seem a little out of control," Braxton said as we strolled along. I could feel his dragon hovering close to the surface. "I thought your energy had calmed since the true mate bond."

I didn't answer immediately. I hadn't forgotten the way Braxton had called me "brother" when I was filled with darkness. The fact that he had finally accepted me into his pack meant a lot to me, because Braxton did not do that lightly.

"The darkness is contained," I told him. "But my emotions are a mess. The true mate bond might have saved the world, but it's also not something I want or need in my life. Tee... It was her sister that I chose as a mate, that I settled with, that I lost..."

We had so much history between us already. So much pain.

"The mate bond was what drew you to that family in the first place," Braxton said, his intelligence second to none. "You chose wrong. Now it's time to make it right."

The dragon shifter saw so much of life in black and white, and normally anyone suggesting that Regina was *wrong* for me would have pissed me right off. But now ... now I somewhat agreed.

"That doesn't change the fact that parts of our past almost destroyed us," I said, mulling it over again. "What if embracing this bond is the catalyst to end it all—maybe we're not meant to be anything more than best friends?"

*Liar.*

My inner energy called bullshit on my denial, but I couldn't afford to just run with that notion. Braxton paused then, his eyes unfocused; I recognized the signs of his mental communication with Jessa. "What is it?" I bit out, each word thundering. My power was definitely stronger, darkness part of it now.

He met my gaze. "Lizzie is gone," he said. "Jessa just told me..."

He didn't get a chance to finish. I opened a step-through into my house, appearing right before Jessa.

"Where the hell is she?" I demanded, my hands clenched at my sides. "Where did she go?"

Jessa crossed her arms, not at all intimidated by the power I was throwing around. Which was good, because I would never hurt her. Not now, and I would like to think not even in the throes of being evil Louis. I'd had the power to kill them all with ease, and I hadn't, so that had to mean something.

"I'm sorry, Louis," Jessa said, her expression sympathetic. "She said she needed some time. That both of you needed to think about what you want and need in your life, and you couldn't do that while the bond was pushing you toward each other."

It all made perfect sense. So much logic in what she said, and still it didn't stop the thud of pain in my chest. "What if she's in danger?" I said, sounding dangerous myself. "She needs to be protected at all costs. She's the light keeping my darkness at bay. She could get hurt!"

Jessa narrowed her eyes on me. "Did you tell her you didn't want another mate?"

I opened my mouth to deny it before realizing I'd kind of said that. "It's safer if I don't let myself care too much. Tee already has so much power over me. I have to make sure that my emotions don't get out of control."

"The darkness?" Jessa guessed.

I nodded, just as the door slammed open and a pissed-off dragon shifter stormed in. He didn't say anything to me, just raced to his mate's side and hauled her into his arms. "Keep fucking acting like a crazy sorcerer and I will kill you, Louis," he said over Jessa's head. She was tucked tightly into his chest. "I trust you with my mate and my pack ... you're family. Don't make me regret that decision."

I didn't bite back, because he had a right to be worried. I was a little out of control at the moment. Jessa twisted in his arms and met my gaze. "A bonded mate is a dangerous creature," I told her softly. "The deeper the bond is, the worse the danger to others. I'm already too powerful. I have darkness in my energy now, no matter what I do. I can't risk any stronger emotions than I already have."

"I don't think it matters," Jessa said quietly. "You already care too much. I think fear is the only thing holding you back, and you deserve the happiness you might find with her. Don't let fear steal that from you again."

Swallowing hard, I let the truth I'd been hiding from finally free. "She's the one I can't ever recover from losing. It was always her. She's my best friend."

Jessa's face softened. "Then don't lose her. Take this second chance."

I started to pace, my senses searching desperately for Tee's energy. Trying to figure out where she'd gone. She wasn't in her Alaskan home, and I figured she wouldn't go straight there because it was the obvious place I'd look.

"I can't feel her anywhere?" I said slowly. There was no step-through here, no residue of her magic, only the lingering dragon energy and a few traces of where Tee had been in the house and … near the back door.

I followed that energy, a nervous-looking Jessa and emotionless Braxton close behind.

Out the back of my home, there were the strongest tendrils of gold. Of original magic.

"Josephina left from here," I murmured, and then I put it together. "And Tee left with her."

Fuck. That meant she was in Faerie, and with the way time shifted, it would be days before she made her way back to Earth. There was no point in following her to Faerie either, because by the time I got there, she could be anywhere. And the energy of Faerie would help her hide from me.

She'd arranged it so I'd have no choice but to spend some time considering what I wanted. My genius of a mate.

My blood boiled at the knowledge that right now she was completely untraceable. Our bond hummed in my chest, as if to remind me that she was okay and that I could check on her through it.

"Use this time to think about what you really want," Jessa said.

"And sort out the problem with the humans," Braxton added. "Our borders need securing. An army of humans is moving toward all supe villages now that the elders have revealed our existence to the world."

Thanks to the television program that was airing night and day on their cable networks, humans had started to surround the supernatural villages. At first it was only the humans who lived their lives half in a fantasy world already: gamers, authors, actors, all of them seeking out the magic they'd dreamed of being true. They'd been camping outside Stratford for the last day and half, and they were mostly calm. But things were starting to ramp up now.

The human government must have done their own investigation into what they were seeing on their televisions, and apparently the threat was now real enough for them to bring out their armies. The US president, who had not been aware of us before this, was declaring us a threat of the highest level.

"Have you spoken to our contact in the government?" I asked Braxton. A lot of humans already knew about us. We had guild members in every government sector.

He nodded. "Yes. He's trying his best at damage control, but now that the president is aware, it's basically out of his hands."

I figured as much, but it was still an avenue we had to explore. "We need a council meeting, one with all of the leaders from around the world. There's still time to reverse it, if I can get enough votes."

This was a mess I started, and I was ready to fix it.

"We can put the call out, but it's going to have to be a quick meeting," Braxton said, already moving toward my front door. "We can't leave our communities unprotected, especially not right now."

"Just tell them it'll take a day, and we'll have our final vote."

Supe leaders were scattered across the world in multiple time zones, so it would take a little maneuvering to get them all together at the same time. But the

Compasses would make it happen. They commanded more respect than they realized.

And I needed this issue sorted out as soon as possible, because I wanted to focus on Tee. For the first time in a very long time, a spark was flaring inside my chest at the thought of tracking her down. Of spending time with her again.

I wanted to know if she still loved flowers, the brightest, most colorful ones she could find. If she still drank Faerie wine on the full moon and ran naked through fields. If she ate more food than someone her size should be able to do without bursting, and laughed the entire time because she found so much joy in it.

I wanted to know her again.

We had been friends for most of our lives, and I was determined that we get back to that place. And maybe, just maybe, we could embrace the bond fully. Because I agreed with Jessa—I was kidding myself thinking I could keep her at arm's length.

She was already ingrained into my soul, into my heart. She had been for most of my life.

## 13

### ELIZABETH TERESA MONTGOMERY II

*S*ometimes it was easy to forget that the few hours I spent in Faerie were days on Earth. I crossed with Josephina, and she then opened a step-through for me to take back to Alaska. My cabin there was small but comfortable. Unlike in my youth, I had plenty of money now. All supes were paid a stipend based on the wealth of American supernaturals.

And apparently they were doing really well.

I didn't use money a lot anymore—magic got me most things. Money was for the human world. You couldn't magic things out of nothing, they had to be pulled from somewhere. So when I built my house, wood had to be available somewhere for me to magic it into my posses-sion. So in some ways it was easier for me just to purchase lumber and have someone build it.

It was the same with food.

Which was why right now I was in town, at the local grocery store, stocking up on supplies.

Condor, Alaska, was a small town. Population 1,200—

most of the time, depending on the seasonal trades. I knew everyone by name and face, having lived nearby for decades. For some reason, none of them really questioned why I never aged, and if anyone ever did comment on it, I just used a little bit of magic to confuse them into thinking this was normal. As far as the humans knew, I was Elizabeth Tanner, who lived out of town and kept to herself—which they appreciated.

"Elizabeth!" Karen was in her sixties and had been working at the local grocery store for at least fifty of those years. "I almost sent someone out to your cabin to check on you. Long time, sweetheart."

I gave her a genuine smile because she was always so kind and caring, but never pushy. She accepted that I had my secrets and would not share, and still treated me the same way.

"Yes, I'm sorry. I should have let you all know I was going to visit family. It was a sudden trip though. I pretty much just packed up and left as soon as I got the call."

Literally one second after I got the call, I'd opened a step-through. Louis had always had that effect on me.

"Well, I'm glad nothing bad happened to you," Karen said as she started to ring up my groceries. "Your boys were here looking for you too," she added as she bagged everything up. "They seemed worried."

My stomach twisted a little. I'd forgotten to call Paulie, James, and Connor. The shifters were pack animals, and I was part of their pack when they roamed Alaska. It was terrible of me not to let them know that I was okay.

"Are they here at the moment?"

She shook her head. "Haven't seen them for a few

days, so they might have headed back home. Hard to tell with those three."

It was hard to tell. They ate a very carnivorous diet, which mostly consisted of animals they hunted—not with guns—so they came to town even less than me.

"There you go, dear." Karen handed me the three large bags. "Hopefully I'll see you at Mary Lou's later in the week."

I smiled and winked at her. "You know it."

Mary Lou's was the local bar, started all the way back in 1912. She was the town matriarch at the time and had wanted an establishment that allowed for socializing, dancing, and great food.

It was one of my favorite places, and if I took a little fey wine with me, I got to let loose and dance the night away. I'd always loved to dance ... and sing. Thursday was karaoke night, and I'd been known to sneak into more than a few of them.

In some ways it was nice to be back home, even if my heart ached at being away from Louis. I had spent years getting past my feelings for him, and now I felt like I was back to square one, with that damn sorcerer living in my head ... and chest. *True mates*. It was almost unbelievable, but it also explained so much about our history together.

A rumbling growl left me, which had someone on the street nearby jumping and swinging their head around. Their focus didn't stop on me, because they assumed there was no way I could have made that sound. They were trying to figure out if bears were strolling the streets again. It wouldn't be the first time wildlife decided to step into Condor.

I hurried on, clutching the bags closer to me. We were

nearing the end of the daylight days, and soon twilight would descend over the area. I didn't mind it, my eyesight easily adjusting to the low light, but it was a depressing time for the locals. Which was when Mary Lou's did the best trade, with everyone looking to escape.

As soon as I was out of the main town, I strode into the forest. My senses detected no one in the vicinity, so I felt comfortable opening a step-through straight to my home. I had too many wards up to land inside—no one could directly portal into my place, not even me.

The moment I stepped inside my cabin, everything lit up. Lights washed warmth across the wood features and benches, the fireplace roared to life, and heat filled the space. Dropping my bags on the kitchen bench, I stripped out of my scarf and jacket, hanging them on a nearby coatrack. The food took me a few minutes to put away, and I was already excited to have some of my favorite junk food in the house. I had the worst kind of sweet tooth; it was almost embarrassing, but since no one lived with me and I couldn't die from eating it, what did it matter?

I'd always been determined to enjoy the things about my life that I could. And now ... now I was going to live life to the fullest. I had almost died. I had found my true mate. Things happened when I put myself out there, and despite the ache of not being with Louis, I was ready to get on with my life.

The old Elizabeth Teresa was back.

Warmth in my chest flared to life, and I rubbed a hand across it. Seriously. Damn Louis! Damn him to hell and back. I really was a bit late for that. He'd been in hell with those demons, and we'd come very close to losing him. My breathing grew ragged and I almost screamed at the sudden pain flaring through me. The thought of Louis dying, of never seeing his cocky, too-beautiful face again, hurt worse than that blast had.

"Liz!" The shout and banging on my door startled me from the panic attack threatening me. "Where the hell have you been, girl?"

Connor. Somehow he always knew when I was back from town. Breathing in and out deeply, I straightened my clothes and hurried across to wrench the door open. I had to look way up to meet his gaze, because he topped out at six foot six, minimum, and was burly like most bear shifters.

"Connor!" I cried, throwing myself at him. He caught me easily, hauling me up against his dark blue flannel shirt.

He hugged me tightly, careful not to crush me with his bulk. Connor was a scary supe. I'd seen him turn other bear shifters who dared encroach on their territory into crying children, running away with piss down their legs. But he never scared me. If anything, I enjoyed having these guys in my life, because they never treated me as anything special. I was not a hugely powerful sorceress to them. I was just Lizzie.

When he finally dropped me to my feet, his face creased into disapproval as he examined me closely. "You had me worried," he rumbled. "We didn't hear from you, and then we get up here and it's like this place had been abandoned."

I scrunched up my face too. "Shit, I know. I'm so sorry. I had a family emergency and I just took off in a rush. I kept meaning to call you, but things were a little ... hectic."

His eyes saw too much, and the longer he watched me, the more severe his expression got. "You look ... different, Lizzie. What happened?"

Straightening, I planted my hands on my hips.

"I feel different, and I'm finally going to take your advice. I'm done with hiding. It's time for me to live my life, Con."

A grin broke across his face, and I was struck by how handsome he really was. Like flawless, with broad, strong features, darkly tanned skin, and electric blue eyes. There had been a *moment* between us many years ago, but we'd both decided it was safer to remain friends. He was a leader of his community back home and would have to mate with another bear, so we could never have had anything serious.

Now that Louis had come back into my life, I was happy we made that decision. And not because Connor was any less handsome—he could literally be a Greek god with his face and body—but because I had been in deep denial over my feelings for Louis. I'd thought I was long over him.

I was a fucking idiot.

"This is the best news," Connor said, "but don't think I missed the way you haven't actually told me anything that happened while you were gone." His smile didn't fade though, so I knew he wasn't too worried.

As I stepped back to let him in, he added, "And you should totally come and live with our pack. You know that we know how to have a good time."

I laughed. "I think maybe you might have *too* good a time, if you get my drift." He didn't deny it.

Dropping his boots by the door, he followed me across to my couch. "Where are Paulie and James?" I asked, throwing a bag of chips and dip on my table. I also got him a beer, while I poured myself a watered-down glass of fey wine. No need to get messy this early on.

"They'll be here in a minute. They were just on the phone with the pack."

I eyed him. "And you didn't have to stay for that?" He was kinda the alpha.

Connor shook his head. "Nah, this was about their women."

Paulie and James had a lot of women. Those two were the free and easy ones of the group, and we were all okay with it. Until they found their mates, true or chosen, neither of them would settle down.

Connor and I chatted for a few minutes, talking about useless shit mostly, but it was nice to catch up. I was tired still, after almost dying and traveling to Faerie and back, so after some time I dropped my head back on the couch and let the warmth of the fire wash over me.

There was a beat of silence, and then he said, "Did your family drama have anything to do with Louis?"

I had spoken to Connor about Louis just one time, years ago. We'd both been shit-faced and maudlin, our conversations moving to deep and meaningful places. He'd never looked at me the same after that, and I think part of him knew I would always love Louis.

A long sigh left me as I stared into the ceiling. The fire was dancing shadows across the large wood beams, and it was lulling me to sleep. "Yeah, it was Louis." I yawned. "He almost broke the world."

Connor rumbled beside me before he reached out and pulled me closer. Supes loved to touch. It was life for us, and everything relaxed further inside of me. "I heard what happened. He's now organizing the council leaders, rallying them to try and reverse the humans' knowledge of us."

There was an interesting tone in Connor's voice, but I was too sleepy to delve further into it. But I did manage to say, "You've always thought that supes should not be in hiding."

My face was pressed into his shoulder now, the woodsy and snow scent he carried soothing to me. It was safe and familiar.

"Yes, I voted for this to continue, but there's another, larger vote coming late tomorrow."

Louis would be very busy until then, because he was going to try to convince everyone this was a bad idea. Which meant he would not come looking for me.

"What if he doesn't look for me?"

I must have murmured that out loud, because Connor squeezed me tighter. "Then he's a fucking idiot and I will beat his ass into the ground next time I see him."

I had to chuckle. Connor could probably take on most supes, but he stood zero chance against Louis.

Bastard.

Sleep stole over me then, and I allowed myself to fall. I trusted my little pack, and knew I'd be safe with Connor here.

Sometime later I was woken by banging at the door. Lifting my head, my cheek felt numb from being pressed against Connor's hard chest. I blinked a few times, realizing there was rhythmic breathing coming from beside me. We'd both fallen asleep.

"Elizabeth Montgomery," James hollered. "Open the damn door."

Untangling myself, I slipped out of Connor's arms and crossed to my door. It swung open to reveal James and Paulie, both of them ruddy-cheeked and smiling like crazy supes. Even Paulie, who had very dark skin, looked flushed.

"Baby girl...." Paulie swung me up into his arms, squeezing me tightly. "We missed you. Don't fucking worry us like that again. Fuck. I almost sent out a fucking tracker for you."

Paulie's favorite word was fuck, and fucking was his favorite activity.

"Put me down, you big asshole," I said, hitting him on the shoulder.

My hand immediately ached and I wished I'd learn not to hit these damn bears. They were all built like tanks. Paulie and James were slightly shorter than Connor, but still close to six and a half feet tall. Paulie had black hair, cropped close to his head, military style. His skin and eyes were almost black, and he was without a doubt too pretty for words. James was all blond curls. He'd be adorable if his face wasn't severely masculine. He was rougher than Connor, but with so much sex appeal that I wasn't surprised women threw themselves at him.

The Lakeside pack bred their bears really well. I was probably a saint for not sleeping with all three of them, but I'd always valued their friendship the most, and sex would muddy the waters. Connor and I were lucky we'd gotten past our thing and become nothing more than friends.

"Where have you guys been?" I asked. Connor and I had been asleep for a while. I could tell by how rested I felt.

"Mary Lou's!" James shouted, and I realized they were both semi-wasted. "Come on, girl. It's 90s R&B, and we know you never wanna miss those nights."

I laughed out loud. "Yes, that's exactly what I need. Give me five minutes to change."

Connor was up now. I caught his eye as I dashed past, and he winked at me. My heart swelled a little, and I wondered if this could be enough for me. The love I had with these three, my family, my pack.

I didn't need Louis. Fuck him. Always breaking my heart and leaving me to pick up the pieces.

I was going to drink and dance tonight, because I needed to forget. I needed that more than anything in this world. In my room I shimmied into a pair of skinny jeans, pulling on some boots with heels. The height was required. Other than that, I just wore a black bra and tank, because it got damned hot in the middle of the bar during these dance nights.

Slapping on a little makeup, I quickly braided half of my hair to keep it off my face while still leaving most of the long length down my back. I had so much hair, it was hard to manage at times.

When I left my room, it was to a chorus of whistles and catcalls. "Damn, baby. Will you marry me?" Paulie asked, reaching out and taking my hands to spin me around. "You are probably the most gorgeous supe I've ever seen."

He sounded sincere. I reached out and patted him on the shoulder. "You should save those compliments for the ladies of Condor."

He threw back his head, white teeth sparkling. "Oh yeah, they're already waiting for our return. Think you can magic us there quicker?"

I shook my head. "Yes, I can totally do that."

Grabbing my coat and a small flask of my wine, I hurried us all out of the house. Our step-through took us into an alley near the bar that was almost always deserted. We strode out into the street, laughing and joking. Stewie was on the front door, as he was most nights. He was a mountain of a man, almost reaching the shifters in height, and he kept the establishment under control.

"Good evening, Miss Elizabeth," he said as we reached the door. "Long time."

I threw him a genuine smile. "Nice to see you again, Stewie. How's it going tonight?"

He chuckled, teeth white against his black skin. "A lot of dancing. Everybody loves some 90s."

Oh yes, give me all the 90s. I'd been a huge fan of that era of music.

*Pony* by Ginuwine was on when we pushed through to the dark room, and I was already starting to sway, because this beat got me every time. Mary Lou's was made up of a large main room with a bar running along one wall ... wood, of course. There were a few tables scattered around nearby, and then there was the dance floor. It took up most of the room, and right now there were a ton of bodies swaying together.

I quickly dropped my coat at the check-in desk, the

boys did the same, and then the four of us ended up in the center of the humans. I took a swig of my wine before I passed it across to the others. Faerie wine was potent; it knocked supes on their asses. It was the best thing for us to get drunk on.

After a few minutes of sharing, we were all dancing together. I slid up between Paulie and Connor, the two of them swaying with me. We used to draw a lot of attention, being one chick and three dudes, but now the locals were used to us and just accepted that we were all together, in whatever means they thought we were together.

Paulie and James still always hooked up with their favorites in Condor, while Connor was more discreet. As if they read my mind, the two man-whores danced away, and soon there were barely clothed ladies pressing into either side of them.

I laughed, and the song changed to *I Wanna Sex You Up,* which was more than a little appropriate for this crowd. Connor tugged me closer, and there was desire in his eyes as they ran across me.

He leaned down close to my ear. "Louis is a fucking idiot," he murmured to me, and my toes almost curled in my boots. Why couldn't I have loved Connor as more than a friend? In some ways it would have been so much easier, even with him being an alpha.

Reaching up, I wrapped my arms around him, pulling him closer to me. "He's my true mate," I whispered, knowing he would hear me even over the noise.

The bear shifter froze, pulling back so he could see my face. "True mate?" he questioned, concern sliding across his face.

I nodded, swallowing hard, the alcohol mist that had been in my head starting to fade. I lifted the wine again and took another drink, needing to *not* feel right now. "Yes, but you remember our history. It's so complicated, and ... I'm not sure what he actually wants."

"You ran away from him?"

Realizing that was exactly what I'd done, my eyes dropped as I nodded. "Yeah, like a chickenshit. I bailed as quickly as I could. I can't be hurt by him again."

I'd been so scared Louis would reject our bond, I'd bailed before I even gave him a chance. Sure, I said that we both needed time, and we did, that wasn't a lie, but I could have stayed in Stratford. I could have still been near him. Fear of him hurting me again was so strong that it almost took my breath away. But at some point I had to stop running.

Connor pulled me into his arms again, and I forced my worries down. Within minutes our bodies were moving in sync. Sometime later, he pulled back. "I'm gonna get us some more drinks."

I nodded, my body swaying even once he was gone. Human alcohol would keep our buzz going, which was good because I'd run out of wine. Some of the local men moved in closer now that Connor was gone, and I hid my smile. They always did this, and it amused me because if any of them knew what I was they would run screaming. Apparently the truth of supes had not reached Condor yet, because no one was questioning us, but it would only be a matter of time.

Would I lose this freedom then too? Would they hunt me from their town?

Someone's hands landed on my hips, and I shrugged

them off. Being small was a bitch at times, because you got manhandled a lot. Which pissed me off.

The hands were back again, and I spun around, but he disappeared before I could remind him that he didn't have any right to touch. James was there, his eyes flickering with anger as he stared down at me. "Stay close, baby girl."

I winked at him, but I did dance closer. Paulie abandoned his chick too, coming back to me, and I once again felt loved. Connor arrived with our drinks, and then the four of us stayed close and danced out the next few songs.

## 14

## ELIZABETH TERESA MONTGOMERY II

*A*fter a few hours I'd almost forgotten about Louis —*almost*—my back pressed to a sexy-ass bear shifter, and surrounded by others. I wasn't usually this wanton with them, but my heart ached, and I needed this night. Louis kept breaking me, and I realized now that my pack put some of me back together.

Warmth bloomed in my chest then, and panic filtered in through the haze of alcohol that was keeping me content. Straightening, I swung toward the entrance and my heart almost stopped. The small breaths I was managing to squeeze in and out sounded harsh to my own ears. *Crazy in Love* started to blast through the room, but I barely heard it as I watched him stalk through the crowd. He didn't move anyone out of the way; he didn't have to, because they shifted for him. His power was flowing around him, not visible like the darkness, but it made my bones ache with the intensity.

Connor noticed my panic first, and he turned with a

growl, placing himself between me and whatever was scaring me.

"No," I whispered, stepping into his back. My hands wrapped around his biceps. "No, you can't take him on... He will kill you."

Connor looked down at me, and then lifted his head to his boys. They stepped up, all three on high alert. Louis didn't care, though, and I wasn't sure I'd ever seen him this furious. His eyes were almost glowing purple, and shivers streamed up and down my body, covering me in goose bumps.

"Who the fuck is that?" Paulie asked.

"Louis," Connor bit out. He knew there was only one supe in the world who could get me riled like this.

My chest ached, as did my arms and legs as I fought against running to the sorcerer. Why the hell did he have to be so gorgeous? He was close to the boys in height and breadth, and if you teamed that with his power, there was no supe more lethal ... or attractive ... than Louis.

"I need to deal with this," I said, wiggling my way between the guys so I was slightly in front of them.

"No. Fucking. Way!" Connor bit out, and I heard the growl of bear in his voice. Multiple hands landed on me as they tried to pull me back.

Louis paused then. He was about ten feet away, and those glowing eyes were locked on me. On the hands touching me. His chest started to rumble, as did the floor we were standing on.

"Let me go," I whispered urgently. "Let me go *right fucking now* or everyone is going to die."

For once they took me seriously and I was released. I

took a step toward Louis, fear keeping me alert and burning away the last of my drunkenness.

"Louis," I said slowly, trying to draw his attention away from the three bear shifters behind me. "What are you doing here? I thought we decided to take some time."

There was the slightest of twitches at the corner of his right eye, and I actually felt like I might pass out from panic. It didn't matter how powerful I was, no one could take Louis on like this. I knew through our bond that the darkness remained under control, but it had left remnants behind, and that made for a slightly darker— even hotter, if that was possible—Louis.

Our standoff was drawing attention, but none of us shifted. I felt like the slightest movement was going to cause an eruption. Louis moved first, prowling across to me, sucking all the air from the room around us. He reached out and touched my throat, almost wrapping his hand around it. "You belong to me," he rumbled close to my ear, and fuck if my legs didn't go weak in that moment as heat flooded my body. "The next man to touch you dies," he warned, lifting his head to stare over the top of me again.

Growls sounded from behind me, and I almost panicked as those purple eyes shifted to my pack. "Don't test me, bears. I will rip you into pieces and not think twice about it."

I growled then, and that drew Louis's attention back to me. "If you touch them ... harm one hair on their heads ... I will make your life hell, Louis. True mate or not, they're my pack, and they're everything to me."

A wave of darkness flickered across Louis's eyes, and on instinct I reached out and touched him. He was so tall that even with my heels I still only reached his pectoral muscles, the hard planes flexing under my fingers. His jaw clenched before he worked it slowly, like he was trying to get himself under control.

"Dance with me," I whispered. Dancing took away my darkness. Maybe it would do the same for him.

He regarded me silently, head tilting to the side as he tried to read me. Slowly, I linked our hands together and started to lead him further into the crowd. The humans were dancing again by now. Connor, Paulie, and James remained on high alert, but when I flicked my head, they relaxed slightly, and following my cue, headed back out onto the dance floor.

*Candy Shop* by 50 Cent blasted out into the room, and I started to move against Louis. At first he was stiff, but then his hands came out and rested on my hips. His grip was almost biting, just short of painful, and I clenched my legs together to stop the ache. I needed to get laid, as soon as possible.

We didn't talk, because there was too much that needed to be said between us. We just danced. I'd forgotten how well Louis could dance; his rhythm matched mine perfectly, sexy, smooth, hands remaining firmly on the small of my back as he pulled me into him. His thigh parting my legs so I could press even closer. Desire flared strongly between us, and I wondered how I could possibly resist him.

I'd never even kissed Louis, but in my dreams we'd done so much more than that. I figured dreams were all I'd get. But he'd come for me. Pretty much the second I landed back on Earth, he was here, and that had to mean something.

Hope was the worst, because I was opening myself up to be destroyed again.

*Don't Cha* was the next song, and this one had the sexy beat I preferred, so I swung around, pressing my ass back into Louis. He groaned, and I looked over my shoulder. "Are you trying to kill me?" he asked, looking pained. But the darkness in his eyes was almost gone now as he continued to calm.

I shot him a cynical smile. "You've been trying to kill me for years. Only fair that I get a little payback."

He moved so fast then that I almost missed it. I was in his arms and my back was slammed against a nearby wall. A throbbing need rocked me, and I wrapped my legs around his waist, pressing my hips into him. His huge body crowded into me, and I let a small moan slip out. I had no defense against him, and he was reacting in a primal way to the fact I'd been dancing with the bear shifters. His face was buried into my neck as one of his hands tangled in the loose strands of my hair.

"I need you, Tee," he breathed into my skin. "I'm fucking losing my mind without you, and the darkness..."

He trailed off, but we both knew what he wasn't saying. He was struggling to fight the darkness again. In that moment, my decision was made. My heart was already destroyed. What did it matter if I let him wreck it a little more? I couldn't say no to him ... because I needed him too. I'd given him the week without me, and he'd still come the moment I returned. That had to mean something.

"Maybe this will help us move on," I lied, knowing I would never move on. "Get it out of our systems."

He almost smiled at that, his lips twisting as he pulled

back to face me. "Not sure that's possible, but I'm willing to give it a shot."

I needed this moment, because I would always wonder otherwise what actually being with him was like. So even if I only got this short time, it would have to be enough.

"Let me tell my guys, so they don't follow us."

I murmured this close to his lips, not really thinking about what I'd just said. Louis's chest rumbled and he slammed his mouth against mine, capturing me so thoroughly that I completely forgot I had anyone else in my life. His tongue dominated me, stroking and stirring the flames that had been flickering in my center since he first stormed into the room. "You have no guys but me," he growled against my bruised lips. "You belong to me, Elizabeth, until I say otherwise."

A small part of my brain protested this dominance he was showing, but a much larger part basically lost all train of thought as desire rocked me. I had never, not even with my sister, seen Louis this primal.

He was claiming me. Devouring me. And I couldn't get enough of it.

When he had thoroughly kissed the hell out of me, he let me slowly slide to my unsteady feet. I wobbled for a moment, and then gained my equilibrium. "Tell them not to come by for a few days," he warned me. I started to move, pushing around him.

"And, Tee..."

I stopped and turned back. "Don't touch them. I only have so much control right now."

That much was clear. His eyes were barely even purple in that moment. If anything, they looked like stormy clouds, ready to lash out and slam chaos down onto the world below.

"Be right back," I promised.

His eyes on me kept that thrum of energy zooming through my body, and I was hyperaware of everything as I moved toward Connor. He had remained on the edge of the dance floor, no doubt watching me closely.

When I neared him, he rushed toward me, and I held out my hands. "Please don't touch me right now. Louis is a little—"

"Unstable," he bit out.

I shrugged. "He's powerful, and that means his darkness is also. He's fighting it, but best we don't push him over the edge."

Connor studied me for a few moments before he let out a sigh. "Are you sure about this?"

Somehow he already knew what was happening.

I nodded, swallowing hard as I rubbed damp palms across my jeans. "I need this moment with him. I need to know what it's like to be loved by Louis."

Sympathy bloomed in Connor's eyes, and I hated that. My voice was harsher then. "Don't come by the cabin for a few days. I'll let you know when he's gone."

His jaw was clenched so hard that I could almost hear his teeth protesting. "Don't let him hurt you, Liz."

I leaned in to hug him, like I always would, before remembering Louis. Pulling back quickly, I just nodded. "I'll be careful. See you three soon."

Connor lifted his head and nailed Louis with a fierce stare, and I had to say, I had never loved my friend more than in that moment. Everyone was afraid of Louis. Everyone in the entire freaking world. Including very ancient and powerful magic users. But for me, Connor risked the wrath of a sorcerer.

"Love you," I whispered, and then quickly spun away before he could say anything.

Louis's face was a storm cloud by the time I got back to him, and I knew he'd heard my last words to Connor, but I didn't even care. He hadn't been there for the past few decades. He didn't pick up the pieces of my life. He didn't give me the will to get back into the world. So he didn't get to be mad because I found a family somewhere else.

This was my new reality, and dark or not, Louis was going to have to deal with it.

## 15
---
## LOUIS

*T*he five days that Tee was off my radar felt like the longest days of my life. Between the humans converging on Stratford, the armies threatening our communities with their weapons, and dealing with council members, I was pretty much ready just to kidnap my mate and hide in Faerie. I spent most of my free time tracking her, just waiting for the moment she emerged back on Earth. I also thought a lot about the future and what I wanted.

And I realized what an absolute idiot I'd been to think I could keep her at arm's length. There was not a minute that she was not on my mind, and my need to touch her, to talk to her, to stare at her beautiful face ... it grew worse every day.

The moment she returned, every spell I'd set up went off, and I knew exactly where she was. Alaska. I'd expected she would return to her home, and I was ready to go straight to her. The darkness inside of me felt out of control, not to a worrying level, but I was definitely unstable without my mate.

"Louis!"

Jessa snapped me out of my head and I focused on her and Jackson, who she was cradling close to her chest. Before I could say anything more, the baby turned his ancient eyes on me and then levitated out of his mother's arms.

"Holy. Fuck!" Jessa whispered as we watched him sail across the room and land in my lap. I met Jessa's gaze over the top of his little head.

"Did you know he could do that?" I asked her, keeping my voice even.

She just shook her head, eyes wide as she stared at her son. A beat later, Braxton burst into the room, looking around as he tried to figure out what had alarmed his mate. Clearly Jessa hadn't shared it through their bond.

"Jackson can levitate," Jessa breathed, turning from me to the dragon shifter towering over her. "He just fucking flew himself out of my arms and into Louis's lap."

The little boy reached up and touched my face, and some of the darkness thrashing inside eased. I hadn't seen the babies since they were born, having been sucked into a demon hellhole on the same night, but the last few days had been a huge comfort as I watched them interact with their very obsessed parents and pack.

The children were special, and I had made the right decision to save them, no matter the personal consequences. "What are you trying to tell me, little one?" I whispered to Jackson, sending out lights of power to entertain him. The kids loved when I created light shows for them. "You think I'm getting a little too worked up?"

Jessa and Braxton were in front of me now, staring down at their son, a mixture of pride and fear in their faces. The unknown was scary, and we had two natural-born dragons in our midst for the first time. The possibilities of what they could do were endless.

"He soothed you?" Braxton guessed.

I nodded. "Yes, the darkness that wasn't suppressed, the parts that will always be in my soul, have been more erratic since Tee left. Jackson's power just calmed them."

I stood, handing the child back to his mother before leaving a brief kiss on both of their foreheads. "But Tee is back now, and I need to go to her. We have a lot to talk about."

First thing we would be discussing was the futility of running from me. We were going to have some very serious words about that. I'd always been a bit of a control freak, but now it was worse. So much worse.

She could handle it though. Tee had always known exactly how to deal with me. We were yin and yang like that.

"Will you be back in time for the meeting?" Jessa asked, cuddling Jackson against her shoulder. "I have a bad feeling about it, Louis. So many powerful supes in the same room. I mean ... everything could go wrong."

I nodded. "Yes, I won't leave you all to face that alone. It's the perfect time to plot death and destruction. I also need to convince the stubborn bastards that my 'expose us all' plan was a terrible one brought about through dark energy pushing me for more energy." Dark energy did not care about possible deaths, as long as it meant more power. My darker alter ego had been willing to sacrifice many in our community, but I didn't feel the same way now.

The meeting would be held in the next thirty-six hours or so, in the Sanctuary of all places, because it was neutral ground. "You know we'll have to deal with the mystics, right?" Braxton told me, his eyes flaring with yellow. "They betrayed us and almost destroyed the worlds."

The mystics definitely had to be brought into line. Their little trick with Grace and her jeweled sisters had been too far. "Except for your brother, of course," Jessa rushed to reassure me. "Quale was nothing but helpful to us, at great risk to himself. I hope they haven't hurt him."

"He's lying low right now." I'd been in touch with him. "But he's not sure how much longer he can stay off their radar."

Luckily, we'd be there soon, and then he wouldn't have to worry about the mystics any longer. As I was leaving the house, I passed Tyson and Grace. Grace had just returned from Faerie, even though her sisters remained there still. She'd been in Faerie a day, no more, and still it had been days away from her mate. I could see how happy they were to be back together—neither of them even noticed me as I strolled down their front porch. They were too wrapped up in each other.

That sort of love was rare, even amongst true mates. It was more than the fated bond, it was genuine caring and respect. They didn't just love each other, they liked each other too. Taking a sharp left, I exited the town and found myself in the forest, not too far from the Compasses' house. I opened a step-through, cloaking myself in warmer clothes as I stepped out into Alaska—blending was important.

Tee had chosen a beautiful area to live in her reclusion, with a small town that I knew she was fonder of than she'd like to admit. I scented some shifters in the area: bears. I'd expected this; I knew they were friends of hers, and somehow during the years I'd kept an eye on her, I hadn't killed them.

Her cabin was high in the hills, very isolated, but her energy was not there right now. Tee was in the town. This surprised me a little. But then, what did I really know about her day-to-day life here? Checking in on her a few times a year and keeping track of her energy didn't tell me about how she lived. I'd missed all of that because I was a stupid, stubborn bastard.

It had been painful though, being near her and not being able to go to her, which was why I never stuck around. The ache of our lost friendship had been as strong as the ache Regina left in my life.

Following her energy, I stopped in front of a bar with bright purple logs lining the outside. A flashing sign advertised this place as Mary Lou's, and I could hear the laughter and music from inside. Tendrils of energy swirled in my center, and I prepared myself for what I was about to see. This was the sort of place that Tee would have frequented in our youth, because she loved to dance. It was one of her favorite things to do, especially when she was sad or angry or hurting. Dancing took her away from her worries.

But was she here alone?

The guard at the front gave me a look, and I knew I didn't have my shit together, but since he was human he couldn't tell how dangerous a creature I truly was. Especially when I stepped through the door and caught sight of her.

She was in the dead center of the room, her head thrown back as she moved her body in slow sensual twirls around the space. She wore tight jeans that showed off her perfect curves, her long hair streaming out behind her in golden lengths.

As a child she'd been beautiful, but now...

She was sexy and fierce and strong and powerful. She was everything I would have wanted and chosen in a mate. My eyes snapped to the three bear shifters that had their paws all over my girl. I could feel the familial ties between the four of them, like a pack...

Which meant I had to try really hard not to kill them.

Even as I had that thought, power flowed out of me and I started to move toward her. The longer I watched her, the more my control frayed. She felt me then, as the bond chimed between us; her head jerked in my direction and all color drained from her pretty face.

The bears reacted to her reaction and tried to stand between her and me, which would have made me laugh if I wasn't basically past the point of all rational thought. She pushed through them, knowing that I could tear those cubs to pieces in seconds if I chose.

When their hands landed on her again, I ground to a halt, gritting my teeth as energy swirled at dangerous levels. She shook them off, and that was enough for me to continue to stalk forward toward her.

My mind was blank as I wrapped a hand around her neck, feeling her soft skin and power flowing beneath.

Words left my lips before I could stop them. "You belong to me."

I felt her compliance and arousal at my words, and hell if my body didn't surge forward. I needed to taste her. I needed to touch her right now. But first I had to warn those fuckers, who were still close enough to hear me.

"The next man to touch you dies." Couldn't make it clearer than that.

Still, they were too stupid to know when the big bad wolf was in their midst. Lifting my head, I nailed the biggest one with a glare. "Don't test me, bears. I will rip you into pieces and not think twice about it."

Tee's panic faded somewhat then as she got protective of her pack. I loved when her eyes flashed as she faced off with me. She'd never been scared of those bigger or more powerful. If anything, that was when she hit back harder.

I barely remembered her argument; I was too fascinated with watching her. And then somehow we were on the dance floor. It took me a beat, but memories of the last time we'd danced like this came back to me, and I reached out and hauled her closer. The music here tonight was perfect for the sort of dancing I needed to do with her, and some of the darkness calmed inside of me. When she turned and pressed her ass into me, a low groan escaped me. My control was shot to shit. I needed to have her now.

In a flash I lifted her, a delicate floral scent smashing my senses as I fought for control. I was rougher than I'd normally be, but she didn't seem to mind as I slammed her back against a nearby wall. Her legs wrapped around me, and even through her jeans I could feel her heat as she rocked into me. *Fuck.*

My head went to the crook in her neck without thought, and I drank in her scent, pressing my lips to the softness of her skin where the tank left it bare. I heard her moan, driving my desire even higher.

"I need you, Tee," I admitted. "I'm fucking losing my mind without you, and the darkness...."

The darkness was unstable without her. Which scared me, because I still wasn't sure if giving in to the mate bond was a good idea, but here in this moment, holding her like this, I knew I couldn't resist her.

When she mentioned "my guys" it was enough for my control to snap. I slammed my mouth on hers, the sweetest taste invading my senses as our tongues collided. She kissed like a fucking dream, even if it was a rougher first kiss than I would have liked.

She blinked up at me, small and innocent, but the fight was not gone. Still, it was clear by the way she was still rocking into me, and the tongue sliding across her lips, that she liked this more dominant side of me. I'd always been careful to lock him down with Regina, in case it scared her off, but deep down ... I was as bad as Braxton Compass when it came to my mate. Dominant. Possessive. Ready to kill.

"Tell them not to come by for a few days," I warned her.

She nodded and started to walk.

"And, Tee..." She stopped and turned back. "Don't touch them. I only have so much control right now."

She bit her lip as she stared. "Be right back," she promised.

I never took my eyes off her, not the entire time. I heard most of their conversation, felt the concern from her friend, and when she told him she loved him at the end, it took every ounce of my control not to stride over there.

I reminded myself that they had been there for her when I wasn't, and that she did love them. But it was me she was leaving with now. *True mate.*

Mine.

## 16

## ELIZABETH TERESA MONTGOMERY II

*L*ouis was silent as we trekked out of town and headed in the direction of my cabin—we could have taken a step-through, but I felt like we both needed a breather and some cool Alaskan air. He didn't seem surprised that I wasn't living in Condor though, and that made me think. "You knew I was here the entire time, didn't you? My wards did shit all to stop you finding me."

I swallowed hard as he met my eyes. It was as disconcerting as always to be locked in that powerful purple gaze. "Of course, I would never leave you without my protection. As long as you were content and safe, I left you alone, because that's what you wanted."

My heart was actually hammering in my chest. I wasn't sure I'd felt like this since the first time I realized my feelings for Louis had developed beyond friendship. That day, and the day he broke my heart by loving my sister, were the two strongest memories I had outside of my family's deaths.

"Why are you really here?" I asked him quietly. "You said you didn't want this bond, that you were too damaged and that another mate might push you right over the edge...."

So why? Why was he doing this to me? Because I had no strength of will to resist him.

He was silent, the only sound our boots as we trudged through the snow. "I couldn't stay away," he finally admitted. "I tried my best, I fought against the urge to follow you, but apparently the selfish bastard side of me is stronger now, and I decided to come and find what's mine. You forced us to be apart for a week, at least for me, and during that time you were the only thing I could think of. You're it for me, Tee. I won't be stupid enough to walk away again. This time I'm going to fight for you."

My knees did that stupid weak thing again, because I had no defense against Louis when he talked like that. This dominant side ... it was literally the hottest thing. Ever. Before I could reply, and I probably wouldn't have been able to speak anyway, he leaned over and hauled me into his arms.

"As much as I love walking with you, is it okay now for us to use some magic?"

I squeezed my thighs together to try to counter the ache he'd started inside of me. "Yes, but you need to let me down. I walk on my own two feet, you know that."

With a grumble he released me, but his hand remained wrapped around my neck as he hauled me closer to him. His strong fingers stroked the muscles there, and I let out another moan.

Fuck, if he could make me feel like this with a simple massage, would I even survive him in the bedroom?

Without thought, because I was almost mindless with desire in that moment, I opened the step-through straight to the front porch of my cabin. Luckily Louis managed to disarm the security system before I got us both fried.

"How?" My mouth was hanging open as we stepped inside. "I spent twenty years perfecting that system."

He grinned, and I sucked in a deep breath. "You did a good job, too, Tee, but you know nothing can keep me away if I really want to be there."

It was true. There was nothing I could do to keep him away from me, and luckily I didn't want to. Not in this moment. For the first time in my adult life, I had Louis all to myself, and he wanted me as much as I wanted him. He'd barely taken his eyes off me since he first strode into the bar, and his hooded stare was heating me like no supe's ever had.

I ran at him, because I was too horny to think of anything but being with Louis in that moment. Screw the consequences, I could deal with them later. That was future Elizabeth's problem.

He caught me with ease, bringing me into his body, and I almost sighed when my legs went around him again.

"Bedroom," he demanded, and I nodded down the hall. The fire was already roaring in the living area, and I knew the bedroom one would be going as well. Louis was thorough.

Our mouths met as he started to walk, and I couldn't help but grind against him. My body was aching. Louis growled and swiped his tongue against mine. When we reached my bedroom, I expected him to drop me down on the bed, but still holding me up with one hand, he reached down between us and worked my tank up and over my head. I leaned back to help him, our kiss breaking as the shirt was flung free. Louis was dressed in far too many clothes for my liking too, and I wasn't patient like him, so I magicked away the coat and Henley he had on, leaving his chest bare.

My eyes ran across the hard planes, all the rigid and heavy lines that spoke of someone used to working hard. His body was perfection, and I couldn't wait to get my mouth on him.

"You keep looking at me like that, Tee, and this is going to be over before it begins."

I laughed, the deep, throaty chuckle spilling from me. "Aw, come on, baby. You've always been an overachiever. I expect at least four orgasms tonight."

His eyes darkened the moment I called him "baby," and I had to admit, it just slipped out, but I wasn't taking it back. I also wasn't taking back the four orgasms thing.

"Your wish is my command," he murmured, and then in a flash I was naked. Both of his hands tightened on my ass. He kissed me again, pushing me back against a nearby wall. I groaned, loving the way he tasted me, running his tongue across mine. He shifted his mouth a little, pressing kisses along my jaw and down to my breasts. He started to lift me then, easing me up slowly as he kissed further along my body, his touch driving me crazy as I moved against him.

I groaned as he lifted me higher and higher, so strong that he showed no strain at all. Eventually I found myself with both legs over his shoulders while I was pressed back into the wall.

"Gods," I breathed, looking down at his head between my thighs.

I expected him to use magic to hold me steady, but he didn't. Just pure physical strength.

*Fuck. Me.*

"Louis," I protested as he pressed kisses to my thighs, moving toward my aching center. "I need to shower first."

He growled against me and his tongue snaked out to taste me. I almost came then, my body tightening at the expert way he slid across my sensitive center. I'd never had a man hold me this way, where I was almost helpless, unable to move. It added another dimension to the sexiness.

"Ready for number one?" he asked, his eyes lifting to trail up the length of my body.

"Fuck. Yes." I moaned, wiggling against him.

His strong hands continued to hold me in place as he lowered his head to me again, and this time he didn't stop. He tasted me over and over, and he knew exactly where to focus to make me lose my mind. I tried to move against him, rocking my hips, but he held me steady, and fuck if that didn't drive me even crazier.

A swirling, needy sensation built until stars flashed before my eyes and I unraveled on his mouth, my body finally able to move as he gave me some leeway. I cried out, over and over, his name leaving my lips as I rode out one of the best orgasms I'd ever had in my life.

Even after I was done, Louis didn't stop tasting me. His tongue was a weapon, and he knew how to use it.

Pretty soon he had me out of control again, and I almost cried out when he lifted his head, those purple eyes glistening at me. "So responsive," he said, before he stepped back, still holding me above him, and then slowly lowered me down until my legs were back around his waist.

"I knew there had to be a benefit of being a short-ass," I murmured, completely breathless.

Louis laughed. "You're the perfect size."

He was perfect.

"I need you," I said, ready to ask for what I wanted.

His smile was slow and I groaned before his jeans disappeared in a flash of magic. We were both naked now, and it could have been weird and awkward, especially since I'd basically just sat on his face, but there was none of that between us.

Tomorrow I'd probably blame the nonexistent alcohol in my system for my behavior, but right now I just wanted Louis.

He lowered me a little further, and the top of his cock teased my entrance. I groaned, wiggling against him. "Holy shit, you're so big," I moaned, pushing myself further down onto him.

His smile was sexy. "You can take me. We were made for each other."

As if to prove his point, my body gave up whatever resistance had been there, and he slid all the way inside. At the current angle Louis was holding me against the wall, he was so deep inside that my center ached. He started to move, slowly at first, and I threw my head back against the wall as the sensations built to their peak.

How was he doing this to me? How could he make me feel so much so fast? "What sort of magic is this?" I asked out loud.

"Not magic," Louis murmured against my neck, his teeth biting down hard enough to leave a mark. "The mate bond. It's beyond all magic."

My body lost control before I could stop it, and I really had been trying to draw out the pleasure as long as I could. I cried out and rocked harder into Louis, while he lifted me higher and slammed into me with force. When I cried out for the third time, his eyes glowed with a murky purple light.

"You're mine, Elizabeth Teresa Montgomery," he said forcefully, leaning even closer to me.

I cried out, the fourth orgasm of the night rocking through me, and by the end I was feeling light-headed as I panted in small gasps.

Louis pulled back from the wall then, turning and walking toward my large bed. He spun around and lowered himself back while I was still on top of him, his hard cock buried deep inside.

"I think we can go five, don't you?" His hands went to my hips then and he lifted me, starting to move up and down.

At first I wasn't sure, but he proved me wrong as his hands gripped me. All too soon, my body responded, and I lost all control, slamming myself down on him as I rode him as hard and fast as I could. It wasn't until right at the end, when I felt the tightening on my center again, those spirals of pleasure rocketing from my clit to my toes, that Louis slowed us down, heavy hands on my hips keeping me in place as he surged up inside of me in long, slow strokes, over and over. And when my world shattered, he groaned and jerked inside of me, over and over, drawing out my fifth orgasm.

I collapsed on top of him, and he pulled me closer, his arms tight around my body. It took me many minutes to get my breathing and pulse under control, because aftershocks continued to rock through my sensitive body. I was going to be sore, even with advanced healing, because he had almost sexed me to death. I was sure of it.

"Come on," he said softly, his hands buried in my hair. He was always touching my hair, and I had to say I liked it a little too much. He lifted us both, our bodies still not separated, and carried me into the bathroom. I was exhausted, my head lolling against his shoulder, and I didn't even jump when the warm water crashed down on me. There was so much unspoken between us, and sex probably shouldn't have been the first thing that happened upon seeing Louis again, but I still didn't care.

"Are you okay?" he asked when he finally lowered me to the ground.

*No.* Nodding, I reached for the body wash. "Yes, I'm great. You?"

He caged me in against the dark tiles of my shower, arms around my head and against the wall. "I know we need to talk," he said softly. "But right now all I can think about is taking you again."

The soap dropped to the ground with a clunk, but neither of us turned away. Instead I reached out and placed both hands on his chest, lifting myself on tiptoes so I could get closer to his lips. He lowered his head to me, and our kiss was slow and teasing. He ran his tongue across my lips and I opened my mouth, allowing him as much access as he wanted.

"You taste so good," he groaned, and I returned that with a groan of my own. "I want to eat you."

I was reminded of him eating me against the wall, and I lowered my hands then, wrapping them around his already hard cock. I stroked him once and then again, and he fisted both hands into my hair, holding me in place. Louis liked to be in control, that much was obvious, and I liked when he dominated me. Most ways, I was strong, but here I trusted him to protect me, so I released my own control.

"Are you too sore?" he bit out, leaning further into my hands.

I shook my head, because I was too turned on to speak. He took me then, slow and strong against the wall of my shower, hot water beating down on us. And I got my sixth orgasm of the night.

I'd definitely underestimated him, and he took great pleasure in proving that to me.

Eventually we got clean, and stumbling out of the shower, I wrapped one of the large towels around myself, my body absolutely spent.

"Sleep," I murmured, and I received a grin in return.

"Get into bed, Tee. I'll be right there."

I didn't really think about the fact that Louis and I would be sleeping in the same bed. We hadn't done that since we were kids, and this time we were definitely not innocent. Sleeping together like this almost felt more intimate than all the sex we'd just had, and I wasn't sure my heart could survive it. At the same time, I wasn't prepared to let him go yet, so I would just have to deal with it. I usually slept naked, because clothes annoyed me in bed, and since we'd just had a shit-ton of sex, I figured I might as well be comfortable.

Once I was properly dry—I used magic on my hair—I

slipped beneath the covers, snuggling into the warm bed. The fire was starting to die down, and I didn't bother to add more magic, because I didn't like my room too hot when I slept.

Despite my nerves over sharing a bed with Louis, exhaustion won out as my eyes fluttered shut and I sank even deeper into the comfortable mattress. Sometime later, the bed dipped slightly and I felt his energy wrap around me.

His power was so strong it followed the damned sorcerer around like an entourage.

My body was tense, despite my half-asleep state, as I waited to see what he would do. A strong arm snaked around my middle, dragging me across the bed and into him. He'd pulled on soft pajama pants, and I wasn't sure if I was relieved or not.

His hand slipped around my front and pressed possessively, his fingers stopping short of the place that ached for him. "Didn't take you for a naked sleeper," he said, close to my ear.

I relaxed back against him, forcing myself not to arch and slide those fingers a little closer to where I wanted them. "Yes, have been for most of my adult life. Clothes are annoying."

His chest rumbled against my back as he laughed. "Fine by me if you want to ditch them permanently. Of course, you'll never be able to leave the house, or have any friends...."

He trailed off and I could tell he was pleased with that suggestion. "Never gonna happen, Louis. You get to control me a little during sex, but in the rest of my life you get no say."

His hold tightened on me, but he didn't reply. I felt the predatory nature taking him over as he staked his claim on me. "You weren't sure about the bond, remember?" I said breathlessly, because his fingers were stroking me softly.

His teeth sank into my shoulder and I shuddered, spreading my legs a little further. He was turning me into a sex addict. I couldn't seem to get enough.

"I want you," he said, so softly I almost missed it. "I'm not sure I can let you go, even though it's the worst fucking idea ever to mate with someone like me. I'm not good for you, for anyone."

"Fuck," I groaned. "I don't want you to be with me just because of this bond."

But if he moved his hand right now, I would kill him. Two fingers slid inside, while his thumb stroked across me.

"It's not just the bond, Elizabeth, and you know it."

I didn't know anything in that moment, because his expert fingers had me in my new favorite place. As he continued to stroke me, my mind turned into a dizzying sensation of pleasure before I cried out, my body tightening around him. When I was done, I let out a low groan and chuckle. "I think it might be safer if I put underwear on at least."

Louis made an annoyed sound but didn't protest when I magicked some underwear bottoms from my drawer nearby. I didn't bother with a top, because that really would annoy me, but I could do panties.

I remembered what Louis had said about the bond, about it being more than that. He'd used my full name, which he only did when he was serious. "We can talk about the bond tomorrow," I said around a huge yawn. I wasn't sure what he did after that, because darkness dragged me under. Apparently all a girl needed for a good night's sleep was half a dozen or more orgasms. Good to know.

## 17

## LOUIS

*S*he slept like the dead, barely stirring even when I pulled her back against me. I was tired as well; the last week had been hell without her, and I'd barely slept. I wanted to just feel her in my arms. To touch her soft skin.

This night had been more than I ever expected. I guess I'd never really let myself imagine being with her, so I shouldn't have had any expectations, but somehow I had. And this blew them all out of the water. She had shattered under my hands, her body so responsive. I was getting hard just thinking about it.

It amused me as well, the way she challenged me. Four orgasms. That would be a short night between us if I had anything to do with it. In her sleep, she turned toward me, snuggling in closer, and my heart did some sort of fucking stupid twirl in my chest. Tee knew how to bury herself under my skin; she'd been doing it since we were children, but it was only now I realized just how deep her hold was.

*You cemented the bond further. What the hell did you expect?*

I'd been too weak to stay away from her, and now, whether she realized it or not, she belonged to me. I would never let her go.

Eventually I buried my head into her luscious hair, which I was probably scarily obsessed with, and sleep dragged me under. I had not slept soundly for many years, since before Regina was murdered, and I expected the nightmares to jerk me from sleep, but I didn't stir until I sensed someone on the edge of Tee's wards. She'd done a very good job at securing her property, and if she wasn't so asleep right now, I knew she would be sensing the alert too. I didn't move immediately, because I knew who was outside, and those handsy bastards could wait a few minutes. Their presence bothered me though, so eventually I slipped out of bed and shut down the ward alarms so they wouldn't wake Tee.

Striding across to the front door, I opened it before I even got there. Three bears stood on the other side, eyeballing the hell out of me.

"What are you doing here?" I bit out, sending power with those words. The three of them flinched, but they didn't move.

The tallest stepped a little further forward. "Elizabeth is a member of our family, and even though she said stay away, I don't fucking trust you, mage. We're here to check on her."

A small part of me was relieved that she had such loyal friends—family, if they thought that—but a larger part of me was pissed off that they were on my mate's doorstep.

Fucking bears.

"She's fine. She's asleep right now, and I would heed her warning to stay away."

The middle one crossed his arms, trying to use his size to intimidate me. Little did he know, I could make the three of them disappear with barely a thought. They were lucky I cared too much about Tee to hurt her like that.

"I want to see her," he insisted.

A rumble rocked my body, and I barely contained the growl. If they thought I was going to let them look at my mostly naked, asleep mate, they were fucking delusional.

"You're treading on dangerous ground, bear. I do admire your tenacity, and I'm grateful for any way you cared for Tee while I was out of her life, but I will take it from here. You can fuck off."

He pushed back at me, even though I could see the wariness in his eyes. He was brave, I'd give him that, but also smart enough to know the predator I was. Especially when it came to Tee.

"I'm not leaving until I see with my own eyes that she's okay," he rumbled, his body changing as the bear took over. His wingmen remained loyally at his side but didn't speak.

"I'm fine, Connor. You can stop worrying." A soft voice broke through our standoff, and I snapped my gaze to her, relieved to see she had pulled on a robe. It was tied tightly around her body, her mussed hair flying around her head. She looked stunning, and I wanted to drag her right back into bed.

She shot a smile at the middle bear shifter, who must be Connor. "I appreciate you checking in on me though."

Connor relaxed somewhat, even though he was still

nailing me with dark glares. "Okay, Liz, we're heading back now. Got to make that big meeting, but keep me updated."

He pulled out his phone and waved it at her, and she nodded. "Yep. Have a safe trip."

The three turned and stomped off, and I spun to face my mate. She lifted her hands before I could move or say anything. "If you even mention once that I have to stop being friends with them, I'm gonna kick your ass right out my door and I will spend the rest of my life figuring out how to ward this place so you can't get in."

Her fire filled my body with energy, and I couldn't stop from stalking closer to her. "You'd succeed as well, I have no doubt." There was nothing she couldn't do when she wanted it badly enough. "I wasn't going to ask you to give them up. I know they're family, but you're going to have to give me some time to wrap my head around it."

She shrugged. "That's fair. I'll allow you time to adjust, until ... whatever this is we are doing ends." Her voice was filled with indifference, but I could see the fear in her eyes. She was truly afraid that I would bail on her, break her heart again.

She was wrong. I'd tasted her now, and I would never have enough.

She must have read something in my expression then that clued her in on my thoughts, because her eyes filled with heat as she took a step closer to me. "The bed is awfully cold right now," she murmured, her teeth pressing against her bottom lip as she stared up at me. The slice of innocence in her almost stole my breath away, and I had to force myself to focus because she was probably going to destroy my mind.

"I was planning on getting right back in," I said, our bodies mere inches apart.

There was desire in her eyes as she smiled. My heart did another stupid swirl, because it was a disloyal bastard and had apparently forgotten the last time a Montgomery tore it from my chest.

Her smile faded as she turned, watching me closely. "Having some regrets?" she asked lightly, taking a step back, her hands tightening her robe. Like that would protect her from me.

Using magic, I lifted her up in a rush and dragged her right across to me. She shot me a narrow-eyed look, and then her energy fought my own, halting her movement. Desire hit me so hard I was near knocked to me knees. She was strong. So amazingly strong. Her power was like a wild, ancient bird, freely flying around the world, untouched.

"It doesn't surprise me at all that you're my true mate," I told her honestly. "If I'd had to list the supe most likely, it would be you. It was always you."

"No!" she cried, and her fight died, replaced by sorrow. It drifted along our bond and I released my power on her, letting her fall gently to the ground. I wasn't sure what had happened, and I wanted desperately to gather her close to me.

But she needed a moment, that much was clear.

When she finally lifted her head and stood tall, her face was clear and her eyes were dry. "It was not always me," she said, cutting through me. "I had to stand on the sidelines and watch you love my sister. I had to stand on the sidelines and watch how much it destroyed you when she died. Regina was everything. It destroyed every fucking one of us!"

She had been left alone. Guilt at my part in that was coursing through me, burning my veins like acid.

"My parents checked out," she said, "and I was pretty sure both of them were happy to die on the battlefield. Anything to be reunited with Reggie. And you ... you were gone. In mind and soul and spirit. The last few times I saw you, I didn't even recognize you. All of you left me. And I rebuilt my life here. I found new friends. Now you want to barge in and start demanding things from me. To start ... making me feel for you again." She took a few steps forward, and she was pleading with me. "Please, no more. I can't do it again. I can't lose you again. I can't be second choice again."

Because I couldn't help myself, I wrapped my arms around her and buried my head in her hair, breathing her in. "I have a lifetime to make it up to you," I said, a seal of promise in my voice. "I can't take the past back, but ... I would, if the opportunity presented itself."

She froze before tilting her head back and meeting my eyes. "You'd take what back exactly?"

Lowering my head, I pressed my mouth to hers. "Everything," I murmured. "I would take it all back ... except you."

It was a truth I had been coming to terms with for a long time now. That what I felt for Regina was strong, but it was not ... enough. We didn't really know each other, we'd fallen into a mateship so quickly, and I'd let myself pretend for some time.

Because she was as close as I could get to her sister.

I saw it now. I had been in love with Tee back then,

but she never indicated she wanted more than friendship, so I'd let myself go for the next best thing. And I had fallen for Regina, that much I would never deny, but my feelings back then were nothing on the roaring surges of emotion that Elizabeth Teresa Montgomery dragged from me every second I was with her.

"You can't mean that?" she said, trying to wiggle down from me. "Remember who you're talking to. I saw you two together. I felt the devastation after she died. Don't lie to me!"

This conversation had been a long time coming. We would never be able to move forward unless we healed from the past. I didn't let her pull free from me though. I couldn't let her go.

"Tee, please, listen to me. I promise I'm not lying. Regina was the substitute for you, she even accused me of it during one fight we had just before she died." Another reason I'd let guilt consume me. "And I mourned not just for her, but for you. I mourned for you, because I lost a chosen mate, but you lost your sister. She was your best friend. And I should have been there to keep her safe."

Tears sprinkled from her eyes before trailing down her cheeks. She was wheezing as she tried to get herself together. "I can't believe you," she cried, and then I was blasted back with her power.

I didn't bother to break my fall, knowing I deserved her anger. My back hit the wall next to her fireplace, but before I could crash through it—and her power was enough that I would definitely have gone through the timber—she pulled me up and dropped me to my feet.

"I need some time," she said, tears still streaming down her cheeks. "I need to visit my sister and my parents, and I need to figure out if I can believe the words you've just given me. If I can believe in us again."

As much as I didn't want to leave her, I knew how stubborn she could be. If this is what she thought she needed, then I would give it to her.

"This time for real, Louis. I'm not kidding."

I nodded. "I understand, this is a lot, but I promise ... I have not lied to you. Not about us. Not about the truth of Regina and me. I need you to know that while I might have panicked in those first few days, I've finally come to my senses. I will fight for this bond, Tee. I will not let you go again."

She buried her head in her hands and soft sobs stabbed me in the chest. The floors started to rock as my power leaked out and energy swirled in my center. If she didn't stop crying, I was probably going to accidentally destroy her house. At least I had enough control to make sure she wasn't hurt in the fallout.

Large silvery eyes were locked on me now, and while tears still poured from them, she was no longer sobbing. "You're so different," she whispered. "Kind of ironic that it took literal darkness to infiltrate your soul before our bond clicked in. I didn't get the light, kind Louis. I get this badass, scary Louis."

I chuckled, taking a step toward her because I couldn't help myself. "I've always been scary, you know that."

She chuckled, her fingertips wiping away her tears. "Yes, you have always been scary, but now there's an edge to you that wasn't there before. A darkness that is part of who you are now, and it makes me wonder why...."

I finished her thought. "Because you're light. You're

the one who keeps my darkness at bay, and unfortunately that's going to be a bitch of a job for the rest of your life, but I hope it's one you decide to take on."

She considered me for a moment. "I want to say yes—every single part of me wants to say yes—but I think I need to deal with my past first. So give me this time."

I nodded. I would try my best not to break my word to her. It was the least I could do.

"I'll be in Romania later today," I said. "At the sanctuary. We're meeting there with all the supernatural leaders around the world. If you have decided by then, I'd love to see you there."

I left it at that, and before she could utter another word, I used magic to speed across to her. Lifting her in my arms, I pressed my lips to hers, just one brief, brushing kiss, and then I set her down before turning and striding out of her house.

In a heartbeat, I had my step-through open and I was gone.

Leaving part of my soul behind.

## 18

## ELIZABETH TERESA MONTGOMERY II

*T*he moment Louis left, a scream rocked through me. Since I knew I was alone on my hill, I let it spill out of me in a roar of emotion. I'd asked him to leave ... to give me time ... again. But now that he was gone, his energy no longer filling every inch of my life, I felt empty.

Weakness invaded my core, and I forced myself to straighten, to magic some clothes onto myself and to do exactly what I'd told him I had to do. I had to deal with my past.

My step-through led me back home, to the place where my sister and parents were buried, to the old farmhouse I had spent my youth in. In Aberdeen, Mississippi. The farm was still mine. I had left it there because I couldn't face it, but I hadn't been able to get rid of it either.

Ignoring the old house, I headed toward the gravesite where my ancestors were all buried. It was right at the far end, beyond the fields of wildflowers. In my absence, everything had gotten unruly. Out of control. And I loved it. This was how nature should look.

Magic kept the grass down around the gravestones, and I paused at the gate, my heart thundering in my chest. I had only been back here once since Regina, and that was to bury my parents.

Worst fucking daughter and sister ever—but it hurt too much to know they were truly gone from my life. Before I could enter, I found myself hesitating and then turning away. I started to run through the fields, like I had as a child, my hands brushing across the flowers.

My favorite old tree was still in its spot, shading the world, and I crawled up onto its thick roots and watched the clouds. Louis used to find me here all the time. All of the millions of times he had comforted me, protected me, stuck up for me against bullies....

Even before we had power, I was always the poor supe, the wild one who didn't follow rules and liked to dress in bright colors. Regina fit in better, but she was still always a little on the outside. People were very critical of social standings back when we were kids.

Memories assaulted me, memories I'd locked down tight and refused to let out for many years. But being here, the same scents, my favorite tree, the home I'd run from, it released the vault.

One of the strongest to hit me, outside of the first day I met Louis and the day my sister and parents died, was the day he told me he was going on a date with Regina. I'd just gotten out of supe college, and was sprawled back under this tree....

*"Tee!"*

*My head lifted at the shout and I looked around for him.*

*Louis's flushed face came into view moments later, and I almost lifted a hand to my chest to calm my heart. How my best friend could affect me like this was insane. But it was getting stronger.*

*When he reached me, he pulled me to my feet in a single strong tug. He was filled out now, towering over me, his broad shoulders square and strong.*

*"She said yes!"*

*I blinked at him, something dark slithering through my body and settling with a dull thud in my gut. "Who said yes?"*

*Louis dated, but never anything serious. He was already making waves in our world, so powerful, so kind, and probably the hottest guy anyone had ever seen. It doubly helped that his family were rich and powerful. He came from blue bloodlines, and it was astonishing that we'd remained best friends through all of that.*

*He eyed me closely, some of his excitement fading. "Regina, of course. You encouraged me to ask her out, remember?"*

*It took everything inside of me not to cry then, because I'd been half joking that day, when Louis had said he was going to join my family one day. He loved my parents and was very excited to be invited into our lives. I'd joked that he'd have to choose my sister as a mate for that to happen.*

The memory faded and I jerked my head up from the roots. The day I'd told Louis he'd have to choose my sister as a mate, he'd given me a dark look. I hadn't known what bothered him at the time, but now I wondered if maybe he'd been hinting at something to do with me. And I'd pushed him to Regina, making it very clear that I was not interested.

Which couldn't have been further from the truth, but I'd been afraid that my desire to have him in my life and family would be clearly written across my face, so I'd gone the opposite way. Like the stupid moron I was.

Pulling my phone out, a long-neglected piece of technology that I rarely had reason to use, I found Louis's number. I'd had it for years. It had felt like a lifeline to him even though I'd never used it.

*Me: When you told me that day you wanted to join my family, and I suggested you'd have to be a chosen mate to Regina, was that the moment I lost you?*

I had no idea why I was asking him this; he probably didn't even remember that day.

His reply was almost instant: *You never lost me.*

My fingers flew over the buttons as I tried to write as fast as my furious thoughts were coming.

*Me: That was the moment though that you went to my sister. Did we have a chance? Was it me you wanted first?*

*Louis: Yes.*

Yes!

My phone vibrated in my hands again and I almost held my breath as I read his message.

*Louis: I miss you.*

Holy shit.

Another vibration. *Louis: I've missed you for years.*

Me too, Louis.

Hugging the phone to my chest, I tried not to cry again. Crying was not productive, and it did not help me deal with these emotions weighing me down. I still wasn't ready to face my family though. It was hard enough just being back here after so many years, so instead I headed toward the farmhouse.

Maybe tomorrow I'd be stronger. Be able to deal.

Once inside, I took my time running my hands across

the dusty wallpaper in the living room. It had originally been a sunny yellow, with a field of sunflowers across the bottom giving it a very cheery vibe. Time had aged and faded the scene, but it brought so many fond memories to mind that I closed my eyes and bathed in the familiarity.

The rest of the house was the same. So many memories, some good, others painful. I remembered sitting at the kitchen bench when Louis told me he was taking my sister on a date. And in my small bedroom upstairs when he'd told me that she was going to be his chosen mate. That he would be part of my family.

Those were darker memories, so I sought others. My mom reading to me in the blue-walled playroom. My dad teaching me how to ride a bike on the old road out the back.

A lifetime of memories. I cried more tears than I thought possible as I walked through my house. And through it all, there was Louis. He was the one constant in my life.

He was my one.

Late that night, I used magic to clean the dust from my old bedroom. Getting into bed, I checked my phone and noticed there was a text from Louis.

*Louis: I miss you even more. I feel your sorrow through our bond. Please let me come to you. I need you, Tee, I need to hold you.*

My heart started to beat erratically, and I almost called him then and there to demand he get his ass into my bed. But then I remembered that I hadn't dealt with my family today. The past would always haunt me until I faced it, and I owed Louis and myself that much. If we were going to do this thing, have a *true* true mate bond, then I had to face my demons.

*Me: I miss you too. It's been hard ... there are so many memories here, and almost all of them have you in them. I need another day to deal with everything. I'll find you. I promise.*

His reply was so fast.

*Louis: I will wait for you. Always.*

I put my phone down as a single tear slid from my eye, dropping to the pillow under my head. In that moment I realized that I'd been waiting for Louis. For all of these years, I'd waited....

And now that he'd finally found me again, could I trust that we could make this work?

Exhaustion pulled me under and I slept restlessly, memories and dreams haunting me.

The next morning, puffy-eyed and cranky, I stormed my way out of the house and back toward my family. The journey to the graveyard was quick, and I forced myself past the double gates, stepping inside.

The moment I did, the energy of my ancestors washed across me, and I soaked it up, some of my frazzled nerves calming. The vessel dies, but the soul and energy caged within it do not. My family would have moved on to the next life, I knew that without a doubt, but some of their power would always be here where they lay.

I went to my parents first, kneeling between their graves. "Hey, guys," I said, still calm. "I've missed you both."

And I had. My mom, with her sunshine hair and vibrant blue eyes, had been the best cook in the world;

her apple pie was still my favorite food. She had loved my dad so much, crying every single time he'd had to leave for supe business. My dad had loved her back just as fiercely. We'd been a very happy family. Until we weren't.

My parents had died of broken hearts because they'd given up after Regina, and I couldn't find it in myself to blame them for it anymore. Her death had taken so much from all of us, and I had given up too, in my own way.

"I want you both to know that I love you very much, and I don't blame you. But I am going to have to let you go ... somewhat. The pain and anger that held me prisoner, they can't be in my life any longer. I've decided not to keep living like a shell of a supe. I'm ready for more life, even if that life includes heartache."

It was the truth, and something eased from my chest as a cool breeze brushed across my wet cheeks. I left my hands on the stones at the heads of their graves for many moments, communing with them and the nature of my home, before I finally released them and moved to my sister. She was on the other side of Mom, and I imagined them holding hands in death, neither of them alone. Dad would definitely have Mom's hand on his side, because they were always holding hands.

Theirs was the sort of love I wanted. The reason I held back with Louis now was because I couldn't be a second pick. I couldn't do it. I wanted to be everything, because I was selfish like that. And Louis had been everything to me.

Still was, if I was honest.

"Hey, Reggie," I said, settling in beside her grave, my hands touching the stone, tracing her name. "I'm sorry it took me so long to visit, sister."

I was already sobbing, and I knew this was going to be one of the most difficult things I'd ever done. Confessing my sins to my sister. "See, I kept something from you, something that I should never have hid, and I was too ashamed to face you." I sucked in a ragged breath. "I loved Louis. I loved him so much that when you started dating I actually wondered if I might die from the pain shooting through my chest. Then when I saw him touch you, it made me hate you a little."

The truth tasted bitter on my tongue. It was part of the reason I had exiled myself for so long. I'd hated myself, and that was the only punishment I could figure out.

"I blamed you for something that was not your fault. It was my own cowardice that cost me a chance with Louis, and you were brave in ways I could never be."

A light energy brushed over my hand, and I could have sworn for a moment it felt like someone was holding it. "I hope you can forgive me, Reggie. Because I would give anything to have you back, anything. You were my best friend, my sister, and I will never stop aching from the hole your death left in my life."

I crumpled forward, my throat and chest burning as I tried to breathe through my tears and sobs. Life was so unfair at times, and this was a loss I would never get past.

"I've been so alone, for so many years." I continued to cry, pressing my face to the ground where she lay. "And I still godsdamn love him."

It was a truth that I tried to hide from, deny, push away. But it was like trying not to breathe. Eventually, you had no choice but to suck that air in, and I had no choice but to admit that I loved Louis as much, if not more than, when we were younger.

The energy this time was more noticeable. It wrapped around me tightly, and then I felt her. Her aura was unmistakable. "Reggie?" I said, lifting my head, the feeling of being hugged still with me.

I knew she was there, or some semblance of her power was, and for a moment I let myself feel her. I had my sister back, for the briefest of seconds.

"I love you. I hope you can forgive me."

The pressure increased, and I felt her love in return. She forgave me.

Then she was gone, in a blink of an eye, and I was a mess.

Somehow my phone was in my hand, and I dialed his number because I needed to hear his voice.

"Tee?"

That low rumble of my name choked me up again.

"Tee, are you okay?"

He spoke again, with more urgency, and a bite in his tone that told me he was worried.

Somehow I managed to choke out a few words. "I ... just ... please talk to me."

I felt him calm. Somehow our bond was working completely fine, even if my brain was a mess. "Let me come to you, please. You're killing me. Your pain is ... more than I can handle."

I squeezed my eyes shut because I wanted him here too, so badly. "Soon," I promised him. "But for now, tell me something ... anything. Distract me."

A brief pause, and I sensed he was getting himself together. Pushing down his worry and anger. I expected him to talk about something heavy ... most probably to do with our bond. Instead he said something I completely didn't expect.

"Your hair drives me crazy."

I blinked before a sob-chuckle escaped from me.

"Seriously," he continued, "I have actual dreams about running my hands through it, and how the hell does it smell like wildflowers? Even when we were kids you smelled of wildflowers. I figured it's because you were always out in the fields, but there were no fields in Alaska and you still have the same scent."

Another chuckle burst from my chest. "Of all the things you could have said, you want to talk about your weird obsessions."

His deep chuckle sent chills across my body, and suddenly all I could think about was his mouth on me. The way he held me up, the strength in his arms and body. This was not the time or place for that, considering I was basically sprawled across my sister's grave, so I tucked those thoughts away.

"It made you laugh," he said, and I focused on Louis again. "And honestly, if I'd heard one more choked breath from you, I was coming there, whether you wanted me to or not. I think you overestimate my control."

"I'm with Regina," I whispered, my free hand reaching out to rub across the stone with her name again. "I felt her here with me. I think ... I think she forgives me."

There was a beat of silence and my heart raced at what he might say. "I'm sure she thinks there's nothing to forgive. Your sister loved you, Tee, more than you'll ever know. We both agreed you were the best of the three of us."

"Do you still miss her?"

It was a stupid question, I knew he did, but like all stupid things I think, I had to say it.

Another silent beat. Or a few beats more. "I haven't missed her for a long time, but I still mourn her loss. The world needs more Montgomerys in it. But ... my heart no longer aches for her. When I stopped punishing myself, I realized that I'd moved on a long time ago."

"Could you move on from me?" I wondered, because there might come a time when that would happen.

There was a whoosh of energy, and then Louis was standing before me. He'd magicked himself right into the damn graveyard.

"W-what?" The phone fell from my fingers as I stared up at him.

His eyes examined my face, fingers lifting to brush away the last of my tears. His hands then cupped my cheeks. "I will never be able to move on from you. If you were no longer in this world, then I would follow you to the next one. Not for a moment did I consider it with Regina, but for you there's no other option. I've stayed with you for years, even if you didn't know I was there. As long as you were okay, I let you be. But now ... now that I've touched and tasted and loved you, I cannot leave you again."

He was begging me with his eyes to not push him away, and with a weight gone from me after the moment with my sister, I felt like I could do this. I could give myself to Louis.

"Don't break me," I whispered as I went up on my toes to wrap my arms around him.

His lips met mine in a kiss so fiery that I felt it all the way through my body. It was probably hugely inappropriate to be kissing in the middle of a cemetery, but somehow it felt like another step toward healing. My family was with me in that moment, their love and support almost tangible, and I knew they would be okay with my choices now.

"Are we really doing this?" I said, almost unable to believe it was real. "I mean, so many years, so much history. I can't believe we're in this moment now."

He pushed some of my hair back, his eyes locked on me with that intense thing he did so well. "We wasted too many years. I won't waste any more. I need you, and more importantly I want you."

He hadn't said love, but neither had I. We were still holding back, which made sense considering we were both stepping into something new and crazy and scary. I knew I was important to Louis, and that was enough. He'd kept an eye on me over the years, the same way I had with him. We'd never been able to fully let go.

I would never let him go. Here's hoping I came out of all this with my heart still intact, because something told me that losing Louis *after* having had all of him was not a thing I could come back from.

## 19

---

## LOUIS

*I* had known from the moment I left her place that I was going to break my promise. Leaving her vulnerable and hurting was not something I could easily do, and I fought my baser instincts the entire time, desperate to return to her.

Her face was firmly imprinted in my mind. All of those golden tresses, and her full pink lips that tempted me like nothing else. Silver eyes that could be dark and stormy one moment and icy the next. She knew how to use her words to cut a person down, but she was also beyond kind.

Yep, I was never going to be able to stay away from her, but I would make a decent attempt at it. So I left her in Alaska and headed to Stratford.

"Louis!" Mischa had just stepped out onto the deck. She sounded surprised to see me. "Jess said you were taking off to find Lizzie. I didn't expect to see you."

She had Lily in her hands. The child regarded me closely, and I shot the little one a smile, hoping to ease her confusion. They were still getting used to me, and I knew my power was disconcerting for most people, especially young children. "She needs some time," I said simply. "She thinks we both do, but ... everything is very clear for me now."

Mischa stepped closer, looking so much like her sister and yet nothing like her at the same time. She was soft where Jessa was not, and in some ways I preferred the other twin. Mischa was probably going to say something that hurt, and I'd take Jessa's form of therapy any day.

"Give her the time she needs," she said, giving me the advice I knew was coming but hadn't asked for. "But don't wait too long."

That surprised me, and I regarded her carefully. There was a tinge of pink on her cheeks as she stared back at me. "Maximus was almost too late because he took his time to sort his shit out. Don't make that mistake."

I let out a strangled chuckle. "She knows how I feel now. I made it very clear. She's the one who has to decide if she can let go of the past, because if she doesn't, there may not be a way that we can work through our pain together."

I turned back to stare out into the forest. "I already want to go back to her."

That face, it was haunting me.

I was the maker of my own downfall. As most people are.

More supes joined us on the deck then, and I turned to find myself surrounded by pack ... by family. Even the jeweled princesses were back, all of them feeling just a little more powerful than the last time I'd seen them.

"We're heading out early," Braxton said, crossing to me. "We want to make sure everything is safe there."

"You're taking the little ones?" I asked, staring at Jackson in his arms.

Braxton shook his head. "No, this situation feels too risky. We'll leave them here and just take a step-through back to see them a few times a day."

"They'll be safer here in Stratford," Jessa added.

I nodded. "I can open a semipermanent one for you so you don't have to keep leaving the sanctuary to open a step-through."

The twins' faces lit up, and even the Compasses looked relieved to hear that. It was tough for them to be balancing their parent duties in these dark times we kept facing, and I hoped there was peace on the horizon for them soon. A chance to just enjoy their families.

"It will get easier," I promised, taking in their drawn and weary faces. "They won't always be so small and vulnerable."

Evie slayed me with her too-old-for-a-child eyes, and I wondered if she was vulnerable even now.

"I'm just sick of saving the fucking world," Jessa grumbled. "It's a thankless job, and it keeps happening."

Justice, who was dressed all in black, which brought out the color of her jeweled skin and eyes, nodded. "Yep, I haven't even been part of this world for long, but in the short time since I wandered into a friggin' fairy tale, I've been locked in a cage, sold at auction, locked in another cage, had power and blood drained from me, dealt with a crazy-ass sorcerer, was locked in yet another cage, turned into a jeweled princess, and found out I wasn't human."

Grace scoffed. "Girl, you think you've had it rough.

My family tried to kill me. I still don't know where my mom and dad are, most probably dead, and I was the vessel for a shadow."

There was a beat of silence, and then Justice laughed. "What a competition to win."

The deck erupted in laughter as everyone registered the absolute insanity of their lives right now. It had been a tough few years for all the supes here, but I was determined that the darkness would end soon. There might be slivers left, like those inside of me, but there would be light as well.

If Tee had taught me anything, it was that light always trumped darkness. No matter how strong the dark was.

The twins and Maximus and Braxton took off then, taking their children to their grandparents' house. Those little supes were lucky that they had so much love and support around them. They would never be alone.

When they got back, I had a bag packed, and then it was time for us to head to Romania. The meeting was to take place in less than twenty-four hours, and I wanted to get the lay of what we were facing. But first I needed to check on Stratford's security.

My step-through deposited me right on the edge of Stratford, where the force field that protected our world —and the humans from us—was shimmering strongly. I had been feeling more pressure on it in recent times ... mostly because there were thousands of humans out there at the moment, hammering against the wall, trying to get in. I could hear them—because the force field was connected to me—screaming, chanting, fighting.

The groups outside seemed to be divided between those fascinated by us and the ones who feared us. The second group thought we were creatures of the devil, here to bring about the apocalypse.

Suffice it to say, the human world was a mess right now.

I knew other towns had lost control of their fields when the human numbers got so great that they were overwhelmed. But I was keeping ours strong ... along with the Compasses. Between the five of us, half of America could try and bash our door down. We would be able to hold it.

After I checked everything was stable, I sent some calming magic out into the mass of humans. The violence was ramping up, but I could sense the army out there as well now, and I hoped they would hold off the fighting for the next couple of days.

I mostly hoped the elders, chiefs, and leaders made the right choice at this meeting. Because the world was clearly not ready for our people to be out in the open. Not yet. And more importantly, not like this.

The pack was somber when I returned, and that feeling remained as I opened the step-through into my brother's place. He had it set up so I could enter and leave the sanctuary that way. We'd both figured out how to circumvent the ancient securities, and it was here I would set up a semipermanent step-through for my pack.

Quale didn't even blink as we trooped into his living room, and I wasn't surprised to see sandwiches and drinks already waiting there. He was a nurturer by nature, and I still had no idea why he'd been born a mystic. It didn't feel like the right fit, but thankfully it wasn't something he had to deal with anymore.

"Where are the rest of the mystics?" Tyson spat as

soon as the step-through was closed. "I have a small score to settle with them."

When he said small, he meant fucking huge. They had almost cost him his mate and destroyed the rest of the world in the process.

Quale smiled, and it was not a nice smile. "They vanished a few nights ago. I guess word got out that you guys were returning for this meeting."

Didn't surprise me. They had that weak bully mentality, strong in a group situation, but when faced with much more powerful supes, they ran and hid. My phone vibrated in my pocket then, and I pulled it out to check the message.

I got messages a lot; I was part of a large network that monitored and controlled magical objects. Not to mention we also tracked criminals and handled the legal side of releases back into society. So there was no reason for me to expect the message was from Tee, but somehow I knew it was.

*Tee: When you told me that day you wanted to join my family, and I suggested you'd have to be a chosen mate to Regina, was that the moment I lost you?*

Fuck. That question was actually painful to read, and I had immediate flashbacks. I'd been in love with Tee for some time before that day, but there never seemed to be a right time to broach the subject. I kept waiting for her to give me a sign, but she never did. Well not anything obvious. So then, like a godsdamn coward, I'd decided to just hint at the possibility of me "joining her family" in the hopes she would respond with something, and instead she'd made a joke about me being with Regina. Her words had hurt, because I was sure that if she had even one iota of romantic interest in me, she would never have suggested I choose another girl as my mate. So, yeah, that had been the day I decided that it might be better to stop hinting and just accept that I had a really amazing best friend. To be content with that.

Knowing she would be waiting for my reply, I texted quickly, reminding her that she had never lost me. Not in any true sense. And there was no point in rehashing that part of our past. It couldn't be changed.

For some reason, I waited for an unusual amount of anticipation for her next message. My obsession with her was growing to a worrying level, but I just couldn't find it in myself to give a fuck about that.

*Tee: That was the moment though that you went to my sister. Did we have a chance? Was it me you wanted first?*

That was an easy one to answer.

*Me: Yes.*

Yes to everything she asked. I knew I'd been a bit short with that answer, mostly because I was filled with anger and regret. So I sent another text almost straight after.

*Me: I miss you.*

And then another one.

*Me: I've missed you for years.*

Every minute of every year. I hadn't even realized how consuming the emptiness inside of me had been without Elizabeth. Being back with her now, it was showing me.

She didn't reply, but I could feel strong emotions through our bond. I refrained from writing her again, even though I was still holding my phone like a damn lifeline.

"You coming, Louis?" Jessa asked from the doorway.

Everyone had started to move out, but I was still in the kitchen, frozen.

I nodded. "Yep, be right there."

Shelves rocked around me as my power swelled. Tee's emotions were growing stronger, and there was so much pain and grief in them that my control disappeared in a flash. I needed to go to her. I needed to fucking see her. Practicing every single mental calming technique I knew, I breathed in and out deeply.

"Are you okay?" Jessa was right in my face now, and I focused on her for a moment.

Swallowing roughly, I shook my head. "Not really. Tee is hurting right now, dealing with ghosts of the past, and I can't be there with her."

Jessa's smile was sad. "I love that you call her Tee. It's so different from the formality of her name. It suits her. Even more than Lizzie, and I really like it too."

She was babbling, which was very unlike her, and I figured it was because she wanted to distract me and didn't know how. Reaching out, I wrapped my free arm around her and pulled her in to my chest. "Thank you," I murmured. "For everything you've done."

She squeezed me back tightly, and I could hear the rumble of her dragon from outside, but he didn't venture in. Apparently I was just trustworthy enough now, or maybe it was that I had my own true mate. He knew the strength of that bond.

Following them out to the sanctuary, I tried to ignore the sorrow floating through my bond with Tee. Focusing on the chiefs and elders helped distract me a little, but I was a loose cannon trying to deal with my mate's pain. I should be with her. I needed to be with her.

I sent her one more text that night, needing her to know that she was always on my mind. She replied, and I felt better knowing that it was only memories paining her. Memories she was determined to deal with. Alone.

THAT NIGHT I slept like shit. After a few hours, I pulled myself from the bed and ventured out into the forest near the main town. I let my energy drift from me, releasing some of the darkness, while I thought about Tee. I'd had her in my arms—and bed—for one night, and now I couldn't imagine being able to sleep without her again.

When the false light of this world rose, I ventured back to my room, showering and changing before grabbing some breakfast. Sometime later, when it was early morning back in America, I felt another hot surge of pain through the bond, and I almost blew up a small market stall as I lost control of my energy.

Before anything else could happen, my phone rang.

"Tee?" I said immediately.

She made a choked sound, and everything around me shook as supes watched me warily.

I kept my voice calm though. "Tee, are you okay?"

She choked out some words. "I ... just ... please talk to me."

Some of the tension inside eased because she clearly wasn't in any sort of trouble. I let out a low breath, and the rattling of the buildings slowed as I calmed. I needed to see her. This distance was not good for either of us. "Let me come to you, please. You're killing me. Your pain is ... more than I can handle."

It was worse than my own pain. I would be tortured in

186

the land between for an eternity before I'd have her feel like this. "Soon," she promised me. "But for now, tell me something ... anything. Distract me."

Working hard to push down my own worry and anger, I tried to decide which of the millions of things I could say to her. There was so much unsaid between us still, but I understood her need for distraction.

I went with the first thing on my mind: "Your hair drives me crazy."

There was a pause and then a chuckle escaped from her.

A smile tilted up my lips. "Seriously," I continued, "I have actual dreams about running my hands through it, and how the hell does it smell like wildflowers. Even when we were kids you smelled of wildflowers. I figured it's because you were always out in the fields, but there were no fields in Alaska, and you still have the same scent."

Another chuckle burst from her. "Of all the things you could have said, you want to talk about your weird obsessions."

I couldn't help but chuckle in return. "It made you laugh," I said, before my voice went a lot lower. "And honestly, if I'd heard one more choked breath from you, I was coming for you. Whether you wanted me to or not. I think you underestimate my control."

"I'm with Regina," she whispered, sorrow creeping in again. "I felt her here with me. I think ... I think she forgives me."

I knew her sister well, and she more than forgave her. "I'm sure she thinks there's nothing to forgive. Your sister loved you, Tee, more than you'll ever know. We both agreed you were the best of the three of us."

"Do you still miss her?"

I waited for the pain, because usually it was difficult for me to even think about losing Regina, but ... there were just fond memories of the supe I once loved. "I haven't missed her for a long time." Admitting this truth out loud felt almost cathartic. "But I still mourn her loss. The world needs more Montgomerys in it. But ... my heart no longer aches for her. When I stopped punishing myself, I realized that I moved on a long time ago."

"Could you move on from me?" she asked, and this time the pain was swift and brutal. Before I could think twice about it, I followed her energy and somehow arrived right in front of her. I'd never done anything quite like that before ... it wasn't a step-through, more like ... instant transmission.

"W-what?" she said, her mouth ajar as the phone fell from her hand.

I moved closer, drinking in the sight of her. My heart ached and burned at her red, swollen eyes and tearstained cheeks. I brushed away the last of the moisture, desperate to touch her again. I found myself cupping her face, breathing in everything about her. "I will never be able to move on from you." This was the absolute truth I held in my heart. "If you were no longer in this world, then I would follow you to the next one. Not for a moment did I consider it with Regina, but for you, there's no other option. I've been with you for years, even if you didn't know I was there. As long as you were okay, I left you be. But now ... now that I've touched and tasted and loved you, I cannot leave you again."

Part of me was begging, something I'd never done before in my life, but I'd never wanted anything the way I wanted her.

A million emotions flashed across her silvery eyes, and I felt through our bond the moment she allowed herself to trust in it. In us. "Don't break me," she whispered, lifting herself up toward me.

I'd been dying to kiss her, so I wasted no time in pressing my lips to hers. Fire licked along my body and the energy between us veritably hummed. It was so strong even humans would have felt it.

"Are we really doing this?" she whispered huskily. "I mean, so many years, so much history. I can't believe we are in this moment now."

My eyes flicked behind to the gravestones, to her family cemetery. It had been years since I'd been back here, years since I felt the energy of Tee's ancestors. Of Regina. There were so many memories here, at this farm and in the town where I grew up.

I understood why Tee was so emotional, but for me there was peace here now that hadn't been there before. I pushed some of her hair back, mostly just needing to touch it.

"We've wasted too many years; I won't waste any more. I need you, and more importantly I want you."

She smiled, a bright, brilliant smile, and I had to kiss her again. I wasn't sure what the hell I'd done to deserve this second chance, but I was never going to make her regret it.

## 20

### ELIZABETH TERESA MONTGOMERY II

*H*is kisses were addicting. Like, block everything else in the entire world and make me forget my damn name sort of addicting. Unfortunately, we had run out of time to just sit around and explore this new bond between us. I could tell by the urgency in Louis's voice that this meeting in Romania was not going to be as smooth as he'd hoped.

"They're going to fight me on this," he said. "Some of it is about power, but most of it is about what they think is the next logical step for supernaturals to take. But they're not looking at the bigger picture, the long-term effect of what they're doing. Until now we've still had all the power and control while managing to stay under the radar and not deal with the drama of humans. If we are integrated with the humans, we will take that drama on." He pushed his hand into his hair, sending it up in spikes. "We'll be targeted by them. And I, for one, don't want to spend the rest of my life dealing with humans."

My head was resting against his shoulder, his arm

keeping me close to him. He had barely let me go since we finally saw each other again, and I had absolutely no issue with that. "What's your plan, then? Is there any way that you can put this secret back in its box?"

His chest rumbled under my head, and he let out a long breath. "There's a way. It's going to be dangerous, and most probably won't work completely, but there's still one option left to us. If they hurry the hell up and agree to allow me to try."

I pushed myself up and twisted so that I could see his face. Those arresting purple eyes still stole my breath away just like they had that first day we met when we were children. "I guess we'd better get to the sanctuary, then." The meeting was basically due to start in the next few hours, and while I loved that Louis cared more about me than that, it was a pretty important meeting. He couldn't miss it.

I scrambled to my feet and he followed. Both arms wrapped around me as he pulled me tighter into his chest, and for a moment I wondered how this had become my life. It felt like ... too much. I'd been punishing myself for so long that to finally have something good happen, to finally have this perfect moment in my world ... I kept waiting for it to crash down around me.

I had to stop thinking like that though—this would never work if I was continuously looking over my shoulder waiting for the big bad to hit us. Louis must have felt some of my darker thoughts creeping in through our bond, because a scowl brushed across his face, making it appear even more menacing—and gorgeous —than usual.

"Stop doubting us," he said. "You've known me since we were children. We were best friends for years, and I've adored you since you were a tiny doe-eyed girl with more hair than sense. The fact that you are my true mate as well is just a bonus, because I would have chosen you any day. I did choose you. Despite us getting our wires crossed for a little while there."

His words hurt, but in a good way. He didn't disregard my sister or the feelings that they had shared, but he made it clear that I wasn't second choice to him. I never had been.

I hugged him close as magic roared around us, and before I could blink we were no longer at the farm. I had never been to the sanctuary, though I had heard much about it over the years. I knew it was based roughly on the jeweled lands in Faerie, and that it was designed to house and hide supernaturals from the world. If the council leaders got their way and continued this push for human-supernatural integration, would most of us end up here? Hidden away? Never free again?

I wasn't sure how many supes were usually here— some supes called this place home—but when we arrived there were thousands packing the place. The sanctuary was filled with so much power and energy that as I walked through the town hand in hand with Louis, tingles ran up and down my skin and across my neck.

"When was the last time that this many supernaturals would have gathered like this?" I asked him.

Louis spent a few moments acknowledging people, nodding and shaking hands, before he said, "There was a pretty large gathering when we took on the Dragon King, but that was still nothing compared to this."

Familiar guilt scraped away at my insides, and I wondered if I would ever forgive myself for ignoring that call. Louis's hand wrapped tightly around mine, and before I could blink I was hauled into his body, his hard chest slamming against my cheek. "We're gonna stop this right now, Tee." He was looking so fiercely at me that I lost all urge to argue. I really wanted to climb him and fuse my mouth to his. To taste those full lips. Because it was kinda hot the way he thought he could boss me around. Hot and annoying.

"How the hell did you even know what I was thinking?"

Louis grinned, and it was a slow curling of his lips, which started a slow curling in my center as I squeezed my thighs together. "Because I know you. You were wild but empathetic. You always felt everything so strongly. I knew when you ignored my call that a part of you would be eaten up with guilt. Just like I know that that guilt hasn't gone anywhere."

We'd been apart for so many years, it was easy to forget how well he did actually know me. We'd basically grown into our fundamental personalities together. Louis knew me on a level that no one else ever could. But that still didn't mean he got to boss me around.

"You might know me, but that doesn't mean you get to tell me what to do. That's not how this relationship works, mate, and you need to get with the program real quick."

Years ago I would've stormed off at this point because I was all about the dramatic exit, but I was older and wiser now, and knew that talking through our issues was much better than simply giving in to my anger. Of course, Louis never made it easy for me.

He leaned in closer, his breath washing across my cheek as he murmured, "You love it when I boss you around, and you know better than to think that's going to stop. I told you this on the dance floor, and then again after that: you belong to me." He said those last four words slowly and deliberately, and each one sent me spiraling with need.

Fucker.

He was right, and that drove me crazy. But I loved the dominant side of him. It actually turned me on more than anything else.

Louis seemed satisfied with my response, despite the fact that I didn't actually say anything. No doubt it was written right across my face.

"Come on, love."

He started to move, only pausing when he realized that I wasn't moving with him. Immediately, concern slid across his face. "What's wrong?"

"You've never called me *love* before."

And, yep, I was that girl, having to bring something up because I needed to know. He'd never called Regina love either. I'd never actually heard him tell her he even loved her. He just said she made him happy that he chose her, and that he was finally part of our family. I could only assume that he told her he loved her in private. So I never asked. But now I was asking.

He regarded me carefully for many long moments, supernaturals surrounding us, the noise so overwhelming that it almost felt like I'd been dropped into the middle of a rock concert. And yet I felt like we were alone, just the two of us, in our bubble.

"Trying to get me to admit I love you?" he finally asked, a stupid smirk back on his face.

I shoved him a little, because the asshole was starting to embarrass me. "No, that's not what I'm doing at all. It just ... took me by surprise, okay?"

Everything was taking me by surprise this week. The last month, actually.

I turned to leave, but he captured my face with both hands before I could. "I've already told you that you're mine, that I will kill any man who touches you, that I choose you now and always, that I will risk the very darkness in my soul because I cannot stay away from you. I will risk the world, something that I have never done before, just for you."

He had told me that, that and so much more. I knew I was an idiot. And I was too old to think that I needed to hear those three words from Louis. I mean, "I love you" was such an overused phrase that it barely had any meaning anymore. It was the other things he said, his actions, and the emotions running through our bond that told me everything I needed to know about how he felt.

I placed both of my hands against his chest. "I feel the same," I whispered. "I choose you too."

Turning again, I was once again walking, and once again I barely got two steps before Louis's hands were on me. He swung me up and into his arms. His lips pressed into mine, hard and unyielding. Desire coursed through me as I tasted him. Against my mouth he said, "I love you. I have always loved you. I will always love you."

Even though we had both agreed that those words

weren't necessary, he still gave them to me, and I almost embarrassed myself by crying like a little baby all over him. Somehow I managed to keep most of my emotions at bay as I said, "I've always loved you too."

Regina's face flashed in my mind, and I knew for a second she was there. But for the first time, she wasn't between us.

We got back to business after that, but there was a newfound closeness between us. A comfort that told me some of the hurts from the past had finally washed away. Not forgotten, but no longer important.

The crowds parted for Louis, as usual, and he moved us toward the main platform where the council was waiting. "The official vote isn't for a few hours still," he said, "but I really should do the rounds, chat to some of these stubborn council members, and hopefully sway a few more to our side. I was pretty distracted yesterday and didn't get to see most of them."

I shot him a rueful smile, since I knew I had been that distraction. Despite his words, he didn't move to the stage, and I could sense his reluctance to leave me alone. It was near impossible for him to do the job he needed to do with me hanging off him, though, so I waved him away.

"Go," I said. "I'll be fine. Have you forgotten who you're talking to?"

I could more than hold my own, even with the ancients. He tilted my chin up with his fingertips, his eyes heating as he caressed my lips with his own. "I've never forgotten. You're a little spitfire when cornered. I still have scars on my ass."

I laughed. "Oh, I know." His ass was too perfect not to

stare at, and I'd had him very naked for an entire night. "I probably still owe you an apology for that. But, in my defense, it's not very smart to scare a sleeping witch. Especially one who has just learned a fireworks charm."

He narrowed his eyes on me. "Stay out of trouble, Tee. The fate of every supernatural in here rests on that fact. You get hurt...." He trailed off, but I felt the surge of hot energy along our bond. I felt the darkness.

"Promise," I said, hoping to put his mind at ease. "I'll just wander around and see if I can find some of my friends."

I included Jessa and her pack in that now, along with my bears. For someone who had been isolated for most of her adult life, I was actually doing okay in the friends department.

Louis disappeared into the crowd, but somehow it still felt like his eyes were on me.

"Lizzie!" I spun at the shout, and a smile ripped across my face as Jessa ran up to me. "You're here!" she shouted again, wrapping her arms around me.

"Hey," I said pulling back. "Yep, Louis and I just got here. He's gone to chat with some council members, trying to convince the stubborn supes that they're making a mistake with this plan to integrate the humans into our world."

Jessa pulled a face. "Good luck with that. Brax has been at it all afternoon. I finally suggested he just turn into a dragon and eat them all."

I laughed out loud. "And how did that proposal go down?"

She shrugged. "He wasn't opposed, but he was concerned he'd have to take on even more responsibility in running councils around the world, so he's giving the talking thing one more shot."

We were silent for a moment, supes pushing around us as more of them arrived and hurried to find their friends and family. "The boys were just about to hand back their leadership roles," Jessa said quietly, staring out in the distance. "And then this happened, and now they have to stay strong and united to protect Stratford. To keep our shields up."

She finally turned back to me. "It's a lot, you know, trying to keep the world safe all the time. I mean, I have to leave my children behind because these situations are so dangerous. I don't want to keep doing this."

In the time I'd known Jessa and her pack, she'd always been so strong, so secure and confident. I loved her fight and fire, the way she never took shit from any supe. But now she looked tired and a little beaten, and I hurt for her.

Before I could think about it, I reached out and wrapped my arms around her. "It'll get better, Jess. I promise. Life always has seasons, you know, so I want you to just think of this as a hard season for you and your family. But there are better seasons coming, peaceful seasons when you'll be so bored you'll go out and actively look for trouble."

This was the one thing my age had taught me, probably the only thing I knew better than Jessa. Nothing ever stayed the same.

She hugged me back fiercely, burying her head in my shoulder, and even though she was slightly taller than me, it felt like I was the one holding her together. "Thank you," she whispered against my shirt. "I needed that pep talk."

I patted her back. "It's hard being the alpha. You have to be the tough one, the one that keeps it together for everyone else in your pack."

She cleared her throat, but before she could say another word, a huge shadow washed over us, and I'd half pulled magic for a defensive spell when I realized it was only Braxton. I mean, not that there was anything "only" about Braxton Compass, but he wasn't going to attack us, despite the hard and menacing lines of his face. He looked like an ancient god hell-bent on world destruction.

"Jessa babe?" His voice was a rumble, and his eyes were yellow. "Why are you crying? Why do you have me locked out of our bond?"

She pulled away from me, and I waited for her to sass him, because that was how they usually worked, but she just walked into his arms and wrapped herself so tightly around him that he actually let out a low huff of air.

The look on his face right then almost broke me, because his love for her was so strong that I wasn't sure I'd ever seen anyone look at their mate like he was looking at Jessa.

"I'm okay," she said, her voice low and soothing. "Just had a moment, you know. I miss our babies."

Braxton gathered her up into his body, holding her like she weighed nothing. One of his hands started to trace up and down her body, and he was talking to her, but I couldn't hear what he was saying.

Jessa grew more content in his arms, and the taste of

her sorrow, which had been lingering in the air like the last drops of rain, disappeared.

Pressing a hand against my chest, I tried not to let my emotions run away anymore, but I was so sure I'd just witnessed something more than a true mate bond right there. That was ... more.

They were more.

Thankfully, another distraction arrived before I could embarrass myself and cry. "Lizzie ... about fucking time you arrived."

Paulie had me up and in his arms in a heartbeat, and I hugged my friend tightly. "So glad you guys are here," I said, pulling back so I could see him better. "This is absolute chaos, seriously."

Paulie nodded, and then we were joined by James and Connor. Both of them hugged me close, and Connor spent a lot of time examining me as if trying to find injury on my person.

"I'm fine," I said, slapping his arm. "Louis and I are... We're good. We've been dealing with the past, and I think, maybe, there's a chance at a future for us now."

Connor crossed his arms over his massive chest, muscles bulging out everywhere. "That's good, because I really didn't want to have to kick his ass."

A blast of power sent him shooting back then, his feet skidding about six feet across the ground. "You could try, bear," Louis said casually, strolling in and wrapping his arms around me. "But I wouldn't recommend it."

It didn't escape my notice that Louis had pushed all of my friends a few feet back from me, and I raised an eyebrow in his direction.

"What?" he said, somewhat playfully. "They were

crowding you."

I just shook my head at him before turning back to my guys. "So, where is your pack?" I asked, knowing they would be here with the rest of their bears. I'd been wanting to meet their family for a long time, especially after hearing so much about them.

James pointed across to a low building that looked like it might be a bakery or doughnut shop. "Half of them are eating. The other half are running in the forest."

Shifters needed their freedom.

Noticing Connor still wasn't moving, I narrowed my eyes. "Can you move closer to me?"

He snorted. "I can't move my feet at all, so I'm going to say no."

I spun on Louis. "What the hell do you think you're doing? You can't stop my friends from being near me! You can't stop them from hugging me. We're supes, for fuck's sake." I shook my head at him. "You never used to be the jealous, possessive type ... so what's up with that?"

Louis was no longer smiling, his expression serious but not angry. "You happened. I lost you for more years than I care to think about. The darkness happened. The darkness that is fighting me every moment of every day. Just ... I need time."

Even as he said it, I felt his magic ease, and the guys seemed to relax. "We need a compromise," I said. "Because there's no way you can protect me from the world. I've already been hidden away for years. I refuse to do it again. This is a new season for me. One of freedom."

Louis rubbed the bridge of his nose before he let out a deep breath. "Fine, okay. I understand. I'll work on it, and if the darkness gets to be too much, I'll talk to you about it before I start smashing your friends into the ground."

His gaze shot across to Connor, and I saw my friend nod. They had an understanding, apparently. "Don't you have council members to get back to?" I joked, giving him a little shove.

His lips pressed briefly to mine, and I forgot everything.

"Yep. We're bringing the vote forward a little. It'll start in about twenty minutes."

The guys shot a look over at where their family was, before turning back to me. "We'll stick with you, but Connor will be up on the stage," James warned me. "He has to cast a vote for our pack."

I appreciated them sticking with me, especially since Jessa and Braxton appeared to have disappeared. Probably to the nearest soft ... or not soft surface. "What are you voting?" I asked him.

He arched a brow at me. "I know I said I wanted to bring supes out into the world, but from what I've learned, this was not the way to do it. Pure fucking chaos. And personally, I don't want to deal with humans' bullshit. Maybe one day they'll be able to handle our world, but today is not that day. We don't need humans to know about us yet."

"Yep, no amount of extra tits and ass is worth that," James said, and he actually sounded serious.

I smacked his arm. "Seriously, like you have any issue with that, even when the humans don't know about us."

He shrugged, but didn't disagree with me.

The next twenty minutes passed quickly. We all perched ourselves near the stage. It was good that somehow the stage was half a football field in size, because by the time Connor left and the other leaders from the different packs and cities and prison towns got up there, the number of councilmembers gathered together was huge.

Louis stood in the front, and it appeared he was done trying to chat to the leaders individually. At his side was the Compass quads, and I loved the ease with which they stood there together, silently. There was a trust between those five that spoke of a true family bond, and I couldn't tear my eyes from Louis as he looked out over the crowd.

"You're drooling." Paulie smirked, leaning back against a nearby pole. "Never thought I'd see the day that our little Liz was whipped."

I shot him a derisive stare. "Whipped? Really?"

He shrugged. "If the obsessive stare fits...."

I couldn't really argue with him. I was pretty obsessed with Louis. Not that I'd admit that to the purple-eyed sorcerer though. As if he heard me, his eyes slammed into mine, and I felt that stare all the way to my toes. For a brief moment, my feet were moving toward him, and it was only when a sliver of clarity returned that I stopped myself. Now was not the time to crawl up onto that stage.

He crossed closer, and I swear half the supes on the ground with me stared up at him wearing the same expression I had.

"Popular guy." James laughed, but cut the sound off with a cough.

Louis stood right on the edge of the stage and held his hand out for me. Everyone started to look around, trying to figure out who he wanted. A bunch of women pushed forward, like groupies rushing the stage.

I shook my head, and part of me wanted to stay where I was, but I needed to be closer to him as well. Normally, I didn't throw my power around, but this time I allowed it to leak out a little, pushing supes aside so I could get to my mate.

Anger, confusion, and shock was written across faces as I strolled through, all of them wondering who the hell I was.

"Elizabeth." A sorcerer nearby gave me a genial nod, and I returned that with a smile.

"Frank, it's been so long...."

Frank was from my hometown. Mine and Louis's.

The moment he said my name, I could hear the conversations start up. Not many people knew my face, but a lot of them knew there was a powerful sorcerer named Elizabeth cruising around the place.

I was good at ignoring this sort of gossip, so I just continued forward, my body heating at the way Louis's focus never wavered, not even for a second. There was an ache in my center that only his touch would ease.

When I reached the stage, I stared up at him, and before I had a chance to figure out how to get up on the stage, his magic wrapped around me. I rose into the air to be deposited right into his arms.

"Publicly claiming me, huh?" I asked, pressing closer.

There was an actual hush from the crowd before the noise erupted. Witches screamed, shifters howled, and vampires hooted—horny bastards.

Louis didn't care about any of that though, he just held me tightly and kissed the hell out of me. Holy gods above. The mage could kiss.

He was literally good at everything. Smug bastard.

## 21
---

# LOUIS


*I*'d never stopped to think about why I hadn't been possessive with Regina, especially since I always knew it was a strong part of my personality. I'd just figured that I was busy—I'd had a lot more duties in the supernatural community then—and that it worked best for us if I didn't follow her every move. But Tee....

She showed me the truth. Regina had had my love, but Tee had my love, my heart, and my soul. Even when I was supposed to be talking some sense into the dense idiots gathered on the stage, I found myself drifting to where I could see her better, lingering on her as she laughed with her friends. Thankfully, those three were taking my warning seriously, keeping a decent distance from my mate, which helped me maintain control over my darkness.

When Connor joined us on stage, Tee and the other two moved closer. Our bond tugged in my chest, and I knew I couldn't take the distance between us any longer. I needed her. I needed the world to know she was off-limits. Completely off-limits. For once my power was a real asset. Very few could take me on and win, and for my girl, I would destroy them without thought.

Not that she seemed to notice, but the supes around her watched her. Her beauty—which was special and unique—teamed with all of her power, drew them like moths to a flame. She shone with an inner light and strength that was rarely replicated, even amongst the most powerful.

Moving right to the edge of the stage, I knew I was drawing attention, but I didn't care. It was time for our world to know. I held my hand out to her and she didn't hesitate, coming right for me. A small group gathered under the stage, but I didn't even spare them a glance as I used magic to haul her up to me.

"Publicly claiming me, huh?" she said, her full rosy lips tilting up, changing her entire face. Her smile turned her from beautiful to breathtaking.

I couldn't help myself. Even though I knew she would probably hate this sort of public display, I had to kiss her. It was not just about claiming her, but needing to taste her. The urge was growing stronger with each step we took forward in our bond. We'd dealt with the past, admitted our feelings, and acknowledged the love between us.

The bond was a magic beyond all magics, and it was responding strongly.

I was already thanking the gods for my second chance.

Tee was content in my arms, and I watched for danger over her head while enjoying this moment together. "Louis!" Jestal, a mage from Switzerland, called to me. I turned toward him. His sandy blond hair was in disarray; he was not handling the stress well.

"We're about to start," he said.

I nodded once, and then turned my attention out to the sanctuary. There were thousands out there. Tens of thousands, squeezed into the space, wanting to be in on this historic vote. Never before had we been in a situation like this, one which might change the very fundamentals of our world. It was huge. No one wanted to miss it. The only ones who hadn't been able to make it were those maintaining the securities around our towns. Right now, that was almost as important as this vote.

Tee went to move away from me, but my arm tightened around her, keeping her firmly at my side. I could feel her glare, and even though I really wanted to stare at her pretty pink cheeks, I had to focus.

"Welcome," I boomed, magic amplifying my voice so it echoed out across the world. The noise started to die down immediately, and I gave them a few more minutes to get themselves together.

"We're gathered here today to make a very important decision," I continued. "We need to decide if it's time for supernaturals to step out of the shadows, to reveal the truth of our world to the humans. The spell I cast ... should not have been done, but it has begun the process of integrating our worlds. Already, though, there have been more than a few issues. Violence started strong and it's only increasing, and as more humans become aware of us, it will get worse. If you vote correctly today, I will have a chance at reversing this spell. Of giving us another chance at living undetected amongst the humans."

As far as I could see, wide eyes stared at me, and the

energy simmering across the supes was filled with nervousness and unease.

"Humans fear what they don't know," one of the elders said on the stage, his voice as loud as mine. "Maybe we just need to give them time to get used to us. We might as well continue on now, since the process is already started. There will probably never be a mage powerful enough again to release such a spell."

Thomas from Britain hadn't exactly interrupted me, but it still irritated me that he was already trying to undermine my message. "There could very well be a war before there is peace," Braxton grumbled from nearby, and as always, despite his youth, everyone paid attention when he spoke. "A war that could costs many supernatural lives."

"We've had wars before," someone else argued, Yuko, a female fey who controlled a large part of Japan. "A small war and then peace and power. I mean, this is what we've been waiting for. We don't want to hide in our supernatural communities any longer. We're prisoners. And we're too strong to be thought of as prisoners."

Tee made a small sound, and I realized that I was holding her tighter than ever. With a low, "Sorry," I released my grip on her.

She patted my chest. "It's okay, I can sense your need of me through the bond."

I couldn't let my darkness get out of hand here.

More of the leaders on stage started to speak. "Quiet!" I shouted, power spilling from me with force.

An almost eerie level of silence descended over the entire place. "I think you actually froze their ability to speak," Tee said, looking around.

It hadn't been my intention, but it worked for now.

"We can argue all day," I continued, releasing my mate so I could pace across the stage. "Some are for this, and some are against it, that has been clear from the start. And despite the fact that it was my spell, I was not in my right mind when I cast it, and I will now cast my vote— which is the only thing that matters in this situation. I vote no to integration with the humans. It's not time. We're not ready for another major war. Most of us still remember the wars between shifters and vampires. And the war with the demons. No more."

In the sky, way above our heads, lights flickered and the scoreboard lit up. YES and NO were highlighted, and underneath was a number count. A large 1 appeared under NO, registering my official vote.

"It's time now for all the leaders of our world to cast their vote," I added, sucking back the power I'd used to silence the crowds. "Remember that you have your people's lives in your hands. Think about the long-term ramifications. Think about everything that is at stake, and vote like we all might be dead tomorrow if you make the wrong choice."

*No pressure, you selfish assholes.*

One by one, the leaders spoke a yes or no, and the magic of the official vote I'd started registered it. Every leader had a chance, and even though I heard supernaturals in the crowd murmur their own votes, none of them would count in the official total.

Tee and I stared up in the sky as the numbers rose, and it was close for a long time. Then the YES side started to pull ahead. By only a few votes at first, but soon it was twenty more than the NO.

"Idiots," I muttered, but there wasn't much I could really say. I'd given them the truth, and it was mostly my fault it was all happening, so I would just have to accept this was out of my hands and deal with the fallout.

Then, to my surprise, Tee pulled away from me, and before I could ask what she was doing, she started to speak, her voice magically amplified. "Before you cast your final votes," she said, no inflection in her tone, "I want you all to see something. Because if a sorcerer with the power of Louis is afraid for our future, should we really continue down this path?" She took a deep breath. "I know a lot of you talk about war casually and don't seem to be scared for what that might mean. I also know a lot of you haven't lived through a war, or if you have, you've forgotten it." Her jaw worked for a moment, and then her voice was shaky. "If you have children with you, cover their eyes now."

She lifted both of her hands to the sky, mist pouring from her fingertips. I realized what she was doing, and already I was both angry and sad for her. That she had to do this just to get them to pay attention was really fucking annoying.

She had to relive her pain all over again.

The mist swirled and formed an image very quickly, and then in the sky was a scene, depicted as clearly as it would be on a cinema screen. I recognized the field, even though that was not a battle I'd fought in. It was chaos, bloody and brutal as supernaturals fought against the demon touched. This was clearly taken straight from her memories, and she was running, screaming, trying to find her parents, all the while using her magic in an attempt to save those around her.

I'd been in enough battles to almost taste the bitterness of that day on my tongue, to smell the copper of blood, which would have coated the ground and turned the dirt into red mud—felt the fear as those I cared about were slaughtered around me.

"This is the future you're all signing up for," she whispered. Everyone still heard her though. "Losing people you love. Both of my parents died that day. My mother was raped, and then she was torn into twenty pieces. I know this because I gathered them all up, one by one, and put her back together." She continued on, and I fought my urge to blast this world into as many little pieces as she'd found her mother in. "My father, he was gutted by his best friend. His friend who decided that the power of a demon was more important than eighty years of friendship."

Her voice caught, and I had to step forward. I had to touch her. She welcomed me into her arms, and I closed my eyes while my darker energy pulsed between us. "I'm so sorry, Tee," I murmured through my clenched teeth. "I should have been there."

She pulled me even tighter to her. "I'm glad you weren't. I might have lost you that day as well."

We were in our own world then, and it took me a moment to register the screams and cries from the crowd. The supes on stage were not much better, all of their eyes locked on the scene above, faces turning pale and confused.

Tee noticed as well. "I figured that for a lot of them, they might not have truly lived through a war. Or it has been so long.... The old ones, they forget. They need to understand before the final votes are cast."

She waved a hand above her then, and the scene disappeared in a flash, melting away to leave the sanctuary sky clear again. But I was sure those images would linger in the minds of all. The tally above started to move again, as supes cast their final votes. It was clear straight away that Tee had gotten through to some of them because the NO was now speeding ahead. I wondered, though, if it might be too late. Most of the votes had been cast by the time she spoke up. I still couldn't quite comprehend her bravery, sharing something so personal, and painful, with tens of thousands of supes.

"It's tied again," she whispered.

"Who is left to vote?" someone shouted, and I waited for confirmation of those still required to cast their vote.

"Me," a female said nearby. Her energy felt like vampire. "And I vote ... no."

Uproar and pandemonium ensued, and I hauled Tee closer so she wasn't trampled as everyone moved from the stage. "So what now?" she asked me. "You said it was going to be difficult to bring the spell back. How difficult are we talking?"

I hadn't deliberately hidden it from her, but I knew she wasn't going to be happy when I explained the exact process. It was the only way, though, and this was still my mistake to fix. A mistake that would have been a hell of a lot easier to reverse had they let me deal with it days ago when it first occurred.

"I'm going to have to shift the timeline," I said against the top of her head.

She reacted immediately, lurching back from me, her eyes flashing. "No!" she gasped, pressing a hand to her chest. "No, I won't let you do that. You'll be killed!"

There was a moderate chance that I could be killed, but I also had enough faith in myself and my power to take the risk. Her eyes went wide and shiny, her throat working as she tried to get herself under control. "This is why you changed your mind, isn't it?"

I was taken aback for a beat, wondering where she was going with this.

"Changed your mind about having a mate again. Because you knew you would have to take this huge risk soon, and then we'd be torn apart anyway."

Tears were streaking down her cheeks now, and my energy trembled at my fingertips, desperate to be released. She was killing me, absolutely ripping my heart from my chest.

"No, Tee! This is absolutely not the reason. You're the reason. I need you more than I ever expected to need anything. I will not die."

"How could you strengthen our bond like this," she cried, pushing me hard. "Knowing you're going to kill yourself."

My lips tilted up, and even though I knew it wasn't my smartest move, a small laugh escaped.

She hit me again, her power behind the punch this time, and I actually let out a small oomph as the air was knocked from me. "It's not funny, Louis."

I captured her hand when she went to hit me again. "Always a little spitfire, Tee."

Before she could yell or bite me, both of which she appeared to be considering, I dragged her into my arms. "Why do you have such little faith in me? I'm the strongest mage in the world, and I'm mated to the second strongest. Our bond has given me more energy than even the darkness did. I will not die. There is nothing on Earth, or any other world, that could tear me from you now."

Another choked sob against my chest, but she had stopped fighting me.

"You have some explaining to do, Louis!" another voice snapped from behind me.

I turned to see Jessa, Braxton, and the rest of our pack all there. Glaring. Jessa especially as she stormed forward. "Is Lizzie right? Is there a chance you could actually die from reversing this spell?"

I shrugged. "There's always a chance. I mean, any of us could die at any time, right?"

"No!" Jessa snarled. "Not right. Very, very, not right. We're supernaturals, we're not fragile like humans. We don't die easily. So, I'll ask you again, Louis, what the fuck is going on?"

"Answer her, man," Jacob said from nearby, and he almost looked ruffled as he stared at his best friend. "She hasn't eaten in hours, her kids are not here and we all miss them—and they ran out of cake at the bakery. Something about a group of bears eating it all...."

Tee shuffled her feet, her eyes darting over to where her friends were still standing, watching us closely.

Using my magic, I manifested Jessa the sort of chocolate cake she loved, lots of layers with cream filling between each one, rich, thick buttercream icing on top. "Peace offering?" I said, holding it out to her.

Her teeth snapped together and her nostrils flared a little as she tried not to stare at the cake. "You can't fucking bribe me to forget." Her words had less bite to them this time, and already her focus was wavering.

"We have to have faith in him." Tee took me by surprise when she said this. Not one minute ago, she'd been just as upset as Jessa.

She stepped up to my side, and I wasn't sure my body could contain the new size of my heart as it swelled in my chest. "Since the first day I met him, Louis has been defying the odds. If he says he can do this, I trust him. He wouldn't leave any of us without a fight."

Jessa held her glare for a few more moments, before her rigid shoulders relaxed. She snatched the cake out of my hands, hugging it close to her chest. "If you die," she said, her blue eyes locked on me. "I will track your soul down, and I will torture that fucker for eternity."

"I believe that, and I love you too."

She sniffed at me, and then she lifted the fork I'd added to the plate and took her first bite of cake. Her eyes closed and she let out a breathy sigh. "Holy gods, so freaking good."

There were probably tears in her closed eyes; she was well known for her emotional outbursts over food. Especially cake. Braxton watched her with that look he got, the one that said he would fucking die and kill for her without question. I understood it now. More than I ever thought was possible, I felt the same way about Elizabeth. The supes of this world needed to start thanking their stars that she was alive, because right now she was the only reason all of them were. They should probably thank Jessa as well, because Braxton as a dragon shifter was almost as scary as me.

Almost.

## 22

## ELIZABETH TERESA MONTGOMERY II

*M*y heart had not stopped pounding like a drum in my chest. From the moment Louis had explained his insane plan, I'd been in adrenaline overload. I couldn't quite handle the reality of what he was saying. Shifting the timelines was basically a lesson in ways you should never use magic. We were warned about it from a young age, almost as much as we were warned about embracing our darkness or making deals with demons. A few had ignored these rules over the years, of course, and most of them had died.

It was Louis, though, and I felt deep inside my aching, pounding-too-hard heart that I needed to support him. This was who he was. This was my mate. If there was a way he could save everyone, he was going to take it. I had to just trust in him. He would not leave me easily. I knew that truth more than any other.

"So how can you shift the timeline without shifting everything?" Mischa asked, her arms wrapping tightly around herself like she was chilled.

Louis's gaze flickered to mine for a beat, before he turned back to his family. "That's the part that is difficult. I can't change too many strings of the world's timelines or I could risk affecting a lot more than just this part of the past. I have to specifically find the line where the spell was cast, and I have to change its story only."

"So you don't actually go back in time?" Tyson asked eagerly, wanting more information about this forbidden task.

Louis shrugged. "My ... energy goes back, if you will, and I will possess my past self. I should be able to halt the spell if I take him by surprise. After that, I will return to my vessel ... in the future."

"But changing that could still change everything. Like, will you still be Lizzie's mate?" Grace asked, her hand pressed to her mouth.

Louis pulled me closer, and I could tell her question bothered him. "Yes, we'll still be mates. If all of you are with me when I cast the spell, you should be spared from consequences. And my aim will be to keep all other timelines the same, outside of a few small changes."

He was guessing. There was no exact science to shifting timelines, and there was a reason why this never ended well for anyone who tried it.

"Do the council members know that this is your only option?" Justice moved forward then, less attitude on her face than usual. If anything, she looked a little beaten down, and I hoped everything was okay for her. Outside of this drama.

"They know," he said simply.

Justice shuddered, shaking her head. "I couldn't do it.

You're one brave dude, Louis, and I have no regrets saving you from that demon realm."

He chuckled, and I wondered if it affected everyone else the way it did me, sending tingles across my skin and through my energy. "I appreciate that. But the reality is, this is a mistake I made, and I have to set it right. I won't be able to live with myself if I don't."

Jessa surged forward and wrapped her arms around him. Well, around us both really, because I was still firmly held against his side. "Don't forget how much you have to live for," she said with force and emotion. "I mean it, Louis. Don't forget for even a second, because I bet this spell messes with your mind, putting you back in the world and body where you were dark."

His eyes met mine over her head and I almost drowned in the swirling purple depths. "I will never forget," he said to her, still staring at me.

My heartbeat picked up again, and I sucked air in deeply, trying not to freak out. *Trust.* I had to trust him. It was going to be okay.

"Where are you going to try to shift the timelines?" Braxton asked. "And is there any way for me to help you?"

Louis and Braxton exchanged a look and I saw the same closeness between them that I'd noticed the dragon shifter share with the other Compass quads. I wasn't sure when it had happened, but Braxton had accepted Louis as one of his brothers.

"The dragon might be able to help ground my vessel here," Louis said slowly. I could tell he didn't want to pull any of them into a dangerous situation, and for some reason that calmed me even more. He was taking this really seriously; he was not going to leave without a huge fight. I was finally starting to believe it.

"Done," Braxton rumbled. "I will be by your side the entire time."

"We're going to need to go to the strongest ley line," I said softly. "Louis will need that energy if he's going to stand a chance."

"And where is that?" Jessa asked, looking at me. Then her eyes flicked to Louis. "Please don't say—"

"Antarctica."

"That," Jessa finished. "Ugh, I only just got warm from our last time there, and there is no way those bastards will let us in a second time."

A low voice drifted from across the now almost empty stage; most of the leaders were back on the ground with their people. "You don't need to go into the prisons, so there's no reason for us to say or do anything."

The old supe strolled toward us, his tiny frame hidden under long, thick cloaks. He stood about five feet tall and had tufts of white hair on his head. Most of it had fallen out at some stage. This was a supe at the end of his life, but he still walked upright with strength.

Louis released me and stepped lightly toward the powerful sorcerer. "Lochlan," he said, bowing his head respectfully.

Lochlan waved him away. "Enough of that. We are far past that, my friend."

Louis straightened, towering over his *friend*—I had no idea he knew the famous mage.

"You're the representative from Antarctica?" Louis asked him.

The others wouldn't have been able to leave. That prison required constant power renewal to stay active, and there were too many dangerous criminals in there to take the risk.

Lochlan crossed his arms, the cloak hiding them from view. "Yes, I relayed the vote back to them and the magic recognized that I was speaking for each of our leaders there."

There was a pause, and then he added, "We all voted no. Even before the compelling display from your mate."

His eyes met mine, and it was uncomfortable being locked in his gaze. Not only was he filled with power, but there was so much age and experience in those dark brown eyes, and it made me feel things I wasn't quite ready to deal with.

As if he could sense my discomfort, Louis cleared his throat to bring Lochlan's attention back to him. "I'll be heading straight to the ley line there," Louis said to him. "Please warn the council. I don't want them to lose it like last time."

Lochlan actually chuckled, a raspy sound. "Trust me, Louis, when someone of your power gets close to us and we have no reason to expect it, it's definitely time to worry. We hold the fate of the world in our hands, just like you do, young mage."

Louis didn't argue, he just returned his smile.

Lochlan bade us farewell then, and just like Louis he could circumvent the securities in the sanctuary; he took a step-through back to his prison. Anyone else would have had to leave the walls of this sanctuary to be able to perform magic like that.

No wonder they were good friends.

"We should go now," Louis said, breaking through the silence. "Every minute we wait is another minute I have to go back along the timelines."

Which was why he'd been so angry about them delaying this vote.

Everyone moved forward, and he shook his head. "There's no reason for all of us to freeze our asses off. Braxton and Tee are stuck with me for now, but the rest of you are more than welcome to wait here."

Jessa wasn't the only one glaring, but she was the only one arguing. "No way in this world are you going there without me," she snarled. "I'm going."

Maximus spoke up. "And I'll be there, of course, because Braxton might need the strength of the quad bond. Not to mention, we're all dragons too."

"Right," Tyson and Jacob said at the same time.

Grace's voice was quiet but firm. "Where Tyson goes, I go."

"You all know I'll be there," Mischa added softly. "Max and I are a team."

Louis almost looked like he was going to argue, but he just let out a low breath. "I should have expected that." He turned to the only one who hadn't spoken: Justice.

She was silent for a moment before letting out a long sigh. "Honestly, I don't have anywhere else to be. My jeweled land ... well, let's just say I didn't take to it as quickly as Cam and Gretley took to theirs. They never want to leave. They're already delving into the life and politics and learning their roles. I'm ... at a crossroads."

"It could be dangerous," Jacob warned her, his expression unreadable. He was wearing the fey mask, that perfect shell that hid everything he was really feeling.

I waited for Justice's snap back, because Jacob seemed to rub her the wrong way no matter what he did. Instead, she swallowed hard. "I'm not scared of danger. There are worse things in the world than death. At least that's final, and there's no more suffering to be had. Besides, going out saving the world doesn't sound like a bad way to finish this life."

Jacob's mask finally cracked, just for a split second, but I saw it then, a fury so pure that it was almost scary in its intensity. Flames danced in his eyes, and wind howled across the land. He shut it down almost as quickly, but we'd all seen the loss of control. "You'll come with us," he said coldly. "I need to keep a fucking eye on you, because I don't like your headspace."

Justice flipped him off. "You can get fucked, Jacob. You don't get to worry about my headspace."

He moved so fast that another gust of wind whipped around us, and I couldn't tear my eyes from the pair. Holy hell. The intensity was off the charts. Despite Justice's height, Jacob still towered over her, making her look small. "Getting fucked is definitely a priority of mine," he whispered, leaning even closer to her. Justice sucked in a deep breath, but I heard the small whimper she made. "Even more important is making sure that my pack stays safe. You're part of it now. You will keep yourself a-fucking-live or I will not be held responsible for my actions."

He turned away, releasing her from whatever hold he'd had over her in that moment. She started to frantically suck air in, her eyes wide and unfocused. I felt amusement through our bond and knew Louis and I were thinking the same thing. There was too much tension between those two. Their attraction was intense, and I had no doubt that Jacob and Justice were going to find themselves in a tangle of naked limbs soon. Here was hoping they both survived the encounter.

Everyone gathered close, and I laughed as Justice moved to stand near Grace, putting a wide space between Jacob and her. It didn't matter though; Jacob never took his eyes off the ruby princess, his expression heated.

"All right, I will open the step-through again. I need you all to move faster than you ever have. The sanctuary immediately tries to shut me down as soon as I start, and I can't be wasting power. Not now."

"What about Quale?" Jessa asked, her expression guarded. "Should we tell him what's happening?"

Louis shook his head. "He already knows. He can't leave because he's the last mystic in the sanctuary. He's needed here to keep everything running smoothly."

Quale and Louis had been separated for most of their lives. I'd heard the stories, plenty of times. Louis's family had been rich and powerful, but also cold. It was why he'd spent so much of his life at our house, because he craved the simple love of our family. Money and power definitely didn't give you happiness, not when there was nothing else behind it. It always broke my heart that the brother he should have had in his corner had been so brutally stolen away from him.

I hoped now they would have a chance to develop a stronger relationship.

"He has us now too," Jessa whispered. She was staring at me with a knowing expression. Damn me for never being able to hide my facial expression.

"I'm grateful for that," I told her.

Louis's energy surrounded me, and my body burned

as he pressed his lips to mine. The others moved off the stage, but he stayed there, holding me tightly. "The truth is, I love my family, but you're the only one I need to survive." He said this so softly no one else could have heard it, not even those with extra-acute hearing.

I wanted to cry, but I'd done that a lot lately, and I felt like now was not the time to lose it. I had to be strong for what was about to come. For the huge risk Louis was taking to try to save our world.

"I really wish you didn't have to do this," I said just as softly, and despite my best intentions, my voice cracked.

Regret burned in his eyes. "Me too, love. But you have no idea how determined I am to make it back alive. We deserve a lifetime together, and I will not be robbed of that again."

I needed to hear him call me love at least a billion more times, so I was holding him to that vow.

"Let's do it," I said, swinging around and dragging him off the stage. We got down to where everyone waited, and Louis did his thing and opened a doorway. On the other side, there was a veritable snowstorm going on, winds howling and temperatures at dangerous levels, even for supes.

Louis couldn't waste any more of his energy, so I quickly whipped up a barrier, giving everyone a reprieve from the storm. It was immediately warmer as well, mostly because supes threw off a lot of heat. Especially the Compasses and their dragon souls.

Speaking of...

"Everyone step back," Braxton said, and I could feel the shifter energy washing over him. He shucked off his clothes. Jacob, Tyson, and Maximus followed suit, and suddenly we were surrounded by naked guys.

"People would pay good money for this." Jessa snorted in amusement. "Seriously. I could probably—"

She was cut off by her mate's hand over her mouth, and even though he was smiling, his eyes were flashing heat. Jessa laughed so hard then, and when he released her she actually doubled over.

Her pack watched her with amusement before all four Compasses shifted into their dragons. I managed to widen my barrier just in time, because suddenly it was a tight squeeze inside.

"I'll never get used to that," Justice breathed, her eyes resting on the green-scaled beast closest to her. "I mean, look at them. Have you ever seen something so magnificent?"

Even for those of us raised in this world, dragons were not common, and to see four of them together like this... I understood her awe. I felt it myself.

"I'm going to start now," Louis explained as the dragons lined up behind him. "I will use the dragon energy here to anchor my vessel. No matter what you do or see or feel"—he looked at me on that last word—"you have to promise that you won't touch me. Or any of the Compasses. This is vital. You could be sucked into the spell, and then we'll all be in trouble."

Jessa snarled, but she didn't argue. "Fine," she said. "I promise not to touch you, no matter what."

The others agreed, and then Louis rounded on me. "Tee? Love, I'm going to need to hear you say it."

I shook my head. "Can't promise you that, Louis. And before you say anything, you already knew I wouldn't promise. If you need my help, I'm coming down that timeline."

He wanted to be mad at me—I could see the worry and fear burning in the back of his eyes—but he didn't bother. He knew me well enough to know I could be a stubborn asshole when I dug my feet in.

He just wrapped that hand around my neck again, like he had on the dance floor, possessively taking hold of me. "Worst-case scenario only, you got it? I mean ... you wait until there is absolutely no other option and every possibility has been exhausted."

"That I can promise," I said softly.

He captured my mouth then, the kiss hard and unyielding. Our bond thrummed between us, tinged with desperation. *Trust me.* I swear the words hovered in the air between us, and it calmed me just a fraction. Enough that I could let him go and step back to stand with the girls. I magicked us all coats then, even though it was pretty warm in the barrier, mostly because I needed something to do while Louis started his spell.

I had no idea how he even knew the words that would shift timelines, but I was going to guess he'd studied it in the same book he'd used to bring the human and supe worlds together. I was going to burn that godsdamned book the next time I caught sight of it.

"He can do this," Jessa said, her hand snaking out to hold mine. I could see she held Mischa's on the other side, and Mischa held Grace's. Justice had been a little away, but now she crossed over to me and with barely any hesitation took my other hand. The five of us remained in that line of support as we watched our mates. Our family.

This was going to be a battle for all of their souls,

because the dragons were anchoring Louis, which meant if they slipped there was a chance they'd be dragged into the sea of the past, just like Louis.

All of their lives were at risk, and it was going to be a long wait to find out if they were strong enough.

## 23

### LOUIS

*C*onfidence. Not something I'd ever lacked, which wasn't surprising given my background. My parents had been the worst kind of magic users, arrogant and used to flaunting their supremacy around. Which meant I was raised to believe I was better than everyone else, that nothing I did had any consequences because I was above consequences. If I hadn't met Tee and her family when I was young, I had no doubt I would have been a complete and total asshole as an adult.

Thankfully, she had shown me the light. Called me out whenever I started to grow hubristic. And reminded me that the more power one possessed, the more responsibility they held—the more they should help others, rather than lording it over them.

Elizabeth Montgomery changed me fundamentally, and it was for her safety and future, along with the rest of the supernatural world, that I was now standing in Antarctica about to try and shift a timeline. I'd attempted it only one other time, and I'd been only a few seconds into my attempt before I realized I couldn't bring my dead mate back to life. Timeline shifts were not allowed for that, and if I'd actually succeeded in turning back the time on Regina's death, I would have probably sent the world into a tailspin that would have destroyed it.

Death was beyond my power. Something I had come to terms with a long time ago, despite what I'd thought during the time darkness possessed me.

"Are you ready?" I asked the dragons, my eyes running across the four of them. *Brothers.*

Each of their giant heads bounced. I allowed my energy to flow from me then, trickling down in small waves to the ley line that ran beneath our feet. It was only a trickle, because if I went in full force, I could lose control. There was so much power in this area, it literally had my jaw clenched.

The mate bond thrummed in my chest, and I allowed it to join me. Not enough that if anything happened, Tee would be sucked in too, but enough to keep me grounded. I needed to return to my body here; I had no other option.

Reaching out, I placed a hand on the nearest dragon. To touch one was to touch them all, since they were bonded in a way that went beyond life and death, and immediately that ancient, earthy, foreign magic invaded my body. For a moment I almost pulled away, because dragon energy was … disconcerting. Not something I could easily explain, but I likened it to suddenly waking up in another country, one where the people didn't speak the same language as you. Things were familiar there, but you still couldn't understand anything.

My body started to shake, and I had to move quickly.

Between the ley line, the dragons, and my own power, I was a veritable bomb waiting to go off. There was a spell specifically designed for timeline shifts, and I had memorized it long ago. I couldn't speak through the power, so I just let the words spin across my mind. The ancient language was as familiar to me as English. It was actually my first language, since in my house we spoke it before we learned another word. It did help with spell casting. I'd been able to silently cast since I was very young.

As the words continued to rush around, they exploded into energy themselves, and using the power I held in my hands, I was suddenly seeing more than just darkness in my mind's eye. I was seeing the entire universe. Time itself is not linear. It runs in mad circles and squiggles and loops, showing the infinite number of ways a timeline could have gone. Every decision a person makes changes the path that person is on, even if it's only a small detour.

At first it was beyond overwhelming, the world zooming through my head, the billions of lives and their paths. But breathing deeply, I allowed only those paths where my energy had touched to stay, while sending the rest away. Some of the chaos died off, but there was still enough there to overwhelm anyone. Again, though, I only had to focus on the ones closest to the time I was in now. It had been a week since I cast the last spell, and that had caused such a ripple in my timelines—and in the world as a whole—that it was very clear where I needed to look. The moment I was in the right place, I sent out one burst of warmth to Tee, because this was the moment where everything could go to shit, and I needed her to know that she was my heart. That warmth came back to me with force, and I had to internally smile at my little spitfire. Time had not diminished her fire, and I was eternally grateful for that.

I reached out with my power and wrapped it around a spot in the timeline just before the huge squiggle. Then I was sucked right down that line and ejected into the past. It was disorienting for a moment, while I tried to calm my violently swirling energy. I wasn't supposed to be back here, and the further back one went, the worse it was to deal with. The past was trying to eject me, but I couldn't let that happen. Not until I fixed my mistake.

I was nothing more than a wisp of energy; no one could see me, but I could see all of the familiar faces. I was near the town hall, and past-Louis, with the swirling dark energy around him, had just stormed inside. I followed that energy. My energy.

From the outside looking in, I was astonished to see myself up on that stage: a cruel, mocking smile, eyes hard and cold. I knew I could be a cold bastard at times—I'd cut supes out of my life and turned my back when I shouldn't have—but there was something scary in the mage I had been that day.

The book appeared then, and I realized I was going to run out of time if I didn't move quickly. Focusing only on myself, I ignored everything else in this room, including Tee and my family who were fighting for my soul.

When I reached the front of the room, my energy merged with Louis of the past, and I spiraled into the same sort of darkness that had caused this problem in the first place. This had always been the riskiest part of my entire plan. If I couldn't control myself and the darkness, then I would simply stay merged with this Louis, and if that went on long enough, I would die. Because Louis from the future would die, my vessel that I left there fading away, and then my timeline would end.

Darkness, sticky and unyielding, clung to me as I fought to take control of myself, trying to merge more of my energy into his, to give him some clarity. The internal struggle went on for what felt like hours, and I knew that it would have looked like my body was frozen on the outside, but inside we fought for everyone.

He was so much stronger than I expected. This was my fault. I'd refused to think about this time of darkness, and therefore I did not go into this battle with all the weapons I should have.

Spelled words were coming out of Louis's mouth, and I couldn't lock them down, because I was drowning in the addictive and evil energy consuming my soul. *No. I'm stronger than this!*

My mate bond, something this Louis didn't have, thrummed in my energy. It gave me strength.

The second part of his spell came out garbled as I snapped back with power, not even caring if I had to hurt myself to stop the power. Desperation clawed at me, because I was running out of time. The second part of the spell was finished.

I had managed to delay him though, which changed the timeline, allowing Tee to freeze our power, and for the council members to pour into the room before the spell was finished. I wanted to kill the fucking council members right then, especially the ones who'd blasted Tee, but I had to let all of that happen.

*What if she dies this time though?*

The council blasted out before I could think about it,

and a guttural snarl ripped from my lips as Tee, her beautiful face screwed up in panic, threw herself in front of me.

Before I could even catch her, as I had done that day, I felt pressure on my body in the future—the timelines started to shake as things grew unsteady—and I almost released my hold on the past.

Something was pulling me back, and it might happen before I had a chance to fix my mistake.

## 24

## ELIZABETH TERESA MONTGOMERY II

*T*he moment Louis's energy departed this timeline and traveled into the past, I sagged and would have fallen if Jessa and Justice hadn't kept me standing. "He's gone now?" Jessa asked, urgency in her voice.

I nodded, barely keeping it together. The bond was still in my chest, but it was different, not as strong, more like a wispy tie to the vessel that remained. This was likely because Louis in the past was not bonded to me yet, and now current Louis was back there and our bond didn't know what the hell was happening.

It wasn't the only one confused by it all.

"Braxton said that he's half in the past, half in the present," Jessa whispered.

Grace and Mischa both nodded too. "Yeah, and my mate bond is acting very weird," Mischa added. "It almost feels..."

"Stretched," I finished, and she nodded again.

"Yes, like it's being stretched across time and space."

Which was exactly what was happening. Only for them, most of their mates' energy was still here, whereas mine was very much gone. It was in this moment that I realized how much I truly loved him. I'd been kidding myself to think it had ever gone anywhere. I loved Louis more than I thought it was possible to love anyone. Being with him completed me.

I couldn't lose him again now. I refused.

So I used what remained of the mate bond and tugged on it every thirty seconds, reminding him what was here in the future for him, reminding him that he had to come back to me. There was no other option. After about ten minutes of that, I received something back along the tattered bond—chaos and pure, unadulterated rage. Panic rocked me again, and I wondered what he was experiencing. This time when I tugged on the bond, I poured a lot of my power into it. So much power that there was no way he couldn't feel it.

"Braxton said that Louis needs to get out now," Jessa bit out. "He's been down the timeline too long. He feels the bonds of this future changing."

Braxton was right. The longer Louis messed with the past, the more of the future he risked changing. Frustration and fear hit me hard; I should never have let him do this. We should have just taken the consequences and dealt with the humans.

My mate, always trying to play the hero. If he didn't get his ass back immediately, I was going to hunt him down and murder him slowly. When I couldn't take it any longer, I broke free from the girls and rushed forward. I knew I wasn't supposed to touch him, but desperate times....

"Lizzie, stop!" Mischa shouted, and I briefly hesitated before throwing myself forward. Just when I was about to slam my hands to Louis's chest, the barrier I'd erected around us started to rumble, and all of us were shot backwards, away from Louis. Even the dragons.

Wind, ice, and snow cut into me immediately, and I whispered a spell to protect myself as I tried to figure out what had happened. As I crawled forward, a body came into sight, and my heart stuttered at the sight of Louis sprawled across the ground. Pulling myself up and using magic, I cleared the path to him and ran as fast as my legs could take me, not stopping until I was crouched at his side, gathering him to me. "Louis," I cried, trying to fit his huge frame into my lap but failing miserably.

The bond was still there, so he wasn't dead—it felt the same as when he'd been stuck in the demon world. Something was missing from his body, leaving him nothing more than a shell.

Braxton appeared at my side in his human form, and he looked furious. "Is he stuck in the past?" he shouted, trying to be heard over the storm whipping up around us.

I shook my head and shrugged, my eyes never leaving Louis's still face. I had no actual idea what had happened, and I couldn't get to him in the past any longer because the spell had been broken.

Tears tracked down my cheeks and I let them silently fall, until a surge of heat in my chest had me gasping out loud. "He's back," I said a moment before Louis opened his eyes. Confusion bloomed in them as he blinked at me.

"Tee?" he said softly. "You're okay?"

I narrowed my eyes on him. "Why wouldn't I be

okay?" I choked out. "You were the one risking your soul by going back in time."

He let out a strangled laugh, slowly sitting up. I realized all the others were crowded around us; Maximus in dragon form still was blocking a lot of the elements. "Did you stop the spell?" Braxton asked.

Louis's face went grim. "It was much more difficult than I expected. I didn't remember being so strong when I embraced the darkness of my power, and it was a ... a real fight. I couldn't stop him completely, but I delayed the spell so the council got to him ... and Tee." His eyes met mine and I could see the fury there. Watching me almost die again had not sat well with him. "So there wasn't as much power in the spell, and I reversed it as soon as I knew Tee was...."

"You wouldn't leave until I lived, right?" I guessed.

Louis stood suddenly, lifting me with him like I weighed nothing. He held me close to his chest, his eyes closing as he breathed me in. "If you didn't make it, there was no point in me making it," he murmured to me. "So I fought for us a second time, and I would do it a million times more."

Warm lips pressed to mine, and I forgot everything except my mate. The bond was strong again, thrumming between us like a thick beam of light.

"Uh, guys, can you like make out at home?" Jessa asked, her teeth visibly chattering.

I pulled away, a burst of laughter escaping me. "Oh my gods, I'm so sorry."

I sent my power out again and blocked the cold from everyone, finally able to focus on something other than my mate. "How will we know it actually worked?" Justice asked, looking scared. "I mean, it didn't sound like it went smoothly."

Louis shook his head, hugging me even closer. I rested my cheek against his chest. "It didn't go smoothly, but I definitely shifted the timeline. We won't know the full extent of what happened until we get back to the US. If the humans are still camped outside our communities...."

"What are the chances we made it worse?" Tyson asked, locking Louis in his unflinching gaze. "There's a reason we are warned about using this sort of magic, and while I'm fucking impressed you pulled it off, I'm also fucking worried that we may have screwed the world up even worse."

Louis let out a heavy breath of air. "I'm worried about that too, and that was our only shot. I will not go back again. That part of the timeline will be too convoluted now for me to change it. Once it's been touched once, there's no second chance."

I wouldn't let him do that again, even if there was a second chance. For that brief moment, when he was not quite back with us, I'd died a thousand deaths thinking he would never return. Some of those sadder emotions must have leaked through our bond, because Louis leaned down and whispered softly to me, "Never, Tee, my love. I will never leave you."

"Better not," I said, just as quietly.

When Louis went to open the step-through, I wiggled against him. "I can walk," I said playfully. "This is more a Compass thing anyway, right?" I'd been watching them carry their mates around for days.

Louis flashed his perfect teeth in a sexy grin, but before he could answer, Braxton said, "He's a Compass."

Joy flashed from Louis to me, and my heart actually hurt—in a good way—to know he was finally getting everything he deserved. A loving family. Our true mate bond. And a chance at saving the worlds. Now it was just time to see how the timeline shift actually went, and if we were still facing a battle on our hands.

Louis took us right to Stratford, and as we stepped out, all of us looked around to determine what might have been changed. Judging by the sun high in the sky, it was the middle of the day. I had no idea how long it had been since I properly ate and slept. "Everything looks normal here," Maximus said, with a quick look around.

"Give me a minute," Jacob said as he jogged toward a nearby tree, and in seconds he was gone up it, climbing all the way to the top. The agility of the fey was second to none. Justice's mouth dropped open as she stared at him. "He just, like ... ran up a tree?" she gasped, blinking rapidly. "What in the fuck."

Jessa laughed, but before she could say anything Jacob called down. "Town is still filled with supes, and from what I can see, everyone is going about their normal business."

I was on my feet now, Louis holding my hand tightly, our fingers interlocked. "Let's check the barrier," he suggested, and I knew he was slightly concerned about what we would find. I was nervous, because I had no idea what the supe world was going to do if this hadn't worked.

It took us just under ten minutes to cross the town and

stand before the barrier. It was strong and slightly shimmery, and I could feel Louis's energy threaded strongly through it. He had been helping to power this shield for a long time, most of his life from what I could tell.

"No humans," he said, almost sounding surprised. "They're all gone."

"Next step is to ask someone," I added. "We were all somewhat excluded from whatever changed, so we still remember the previous history. But those who remained behind shouldn't know anything."

Louis closed his eyes and I wondered who he was communicating with. A moment later he said, "Quale knows nothing about our secrets slipping into the human world. He said he's heard nothing."

I was just about to cheer when he froze, his hand tightening on mine. Our connection started to slow, and I almost panicked because he was deliberately blocking me for some reason, but before I could start demanding he share his news, he turned narrowed eyes on me. "It didn't work."

"What?" Jessa gasped from nearby. "What do you mean? The humans are gone."

Louis rolled his broad shoulders, like he was trying to relieve tension in them. "Quale didn't know anything, but an elder here in America did. It appears I only shifted the timeline somewhat. So ... the spell was cut off, and the council did not finish the spell because they didn't have the power when it was so incomplete. But some footage was released to the humans. Only in America. The President of the United States is requesting a meeting."

Braxton made a rumbly sound, which I recognized as his dragon poking its head up. "The president has never known about us, even though we have guild members in the White House."

Louis nodded. "I know, but he definitely knows about us now."

"He probably just wants to make sure we aren't a threat to them, right?" Mischa said, looking around, her arms wrapped tightly around herself. "I mean, that makes sense."

No one said anything, and the worry did not fade from any faces. "We have to check our kids," Jessa finally reminded everyone. "If we're going again, I definitely need to see them before that."

Louis shook his head. "No, you four don't need to go. I'll take Elizabeth. He asked for a few supernatural representatives, so I'll bring Jake and Justice too, for the fey contingent. The rest of you stay here, look after those babies, and we'll keep you updated."

No one argued, even though I could tell they were all uneasy.

Tyson especially looked like he wanted to protest, but we definitely didn't need another sorcerer. Louis and I had that covered.

Jessa hurried over and hugged Louis, and then me, very tightly. "Stay safe. Don't let those humans force you into anything. They don't control us, even if they think they do."

Louis's smile was tight. There was a reason the president didn't know about us, and it had everything to do with keeping our freedoms. I hoped he hadn't risked his life in the timeline jump only for us to find ourselves in a similar or worse position in this new future.

When it was just Jacob, Justice, Louis, and me

standing there, everything felt a little lonelier and a lot heavier. "We're going to take a step-through to a friend near the White House," Louis explained. "We'll wait there until we know what time the meeting is."

"I thought the president already requested it?" Jacob asked. "What's the delay about?"

Louis rubbed at his eyes tiredly. "The president has a lot of requirements and information he wants before we're allowed to see him. Among that is our names, a list of our abilities, and our guarantee that we will not use any of our gifts on him."

Justice snorted. "What the fuck is our word worth to him? I always knew he was a dumbass, but this is next level. Even for him."

Jacob's lips twitched, but he refrained from smiling. She definitely amused him though.

"He might pull out of this meeting when he sees your list of abilities," I joked to Louis, who actually shot me a slow smile.

"I wasn't planning on listing them all. Wouldn't want to scare the poor human."

Because we all knew that this meeting was going to be critical to the future of supernaturals in America. Would the president insist on regulating us, bringing us out into the open? Would he try to control us?

Or would he realize the futility of that and accept that we were beyond his power?

We were going to find out soon.

## 25

---

## LOUIS

*T*here was something the others in the group were not aware of: this was not my first meeting with a president of America. The last one, though, was close to fifty years ago, and he had become a very good friend of mine. He helped establish closer ties with guilds, and especially with placing guilds in positions of power through the US government. The current president, from what I had seen, was definitely not as lenient with his power. He would not be impressed that we had been existing outside of his rule for so long. We did not pay taxes, as we did not use any of the facilities in this country. We were separate, but we did own property and such, so there was some crossover. Again, this was where our guilds came into use, and they smoothed all of the legal stuff that was required.

Blending was definitely growing more difficult as technology improved. These days computers kept track of everything, so we were having to be more careful about covering up our existence.

I had no idea what to expect of this meeting. My time-line shift, which I'd almost not made it back from, had managed to keep most of the world from knowing about us. But did any of that matter if the most powerful and influential man in the country, if not the world, now knew? What the hell would he do with this knowledge?

What price was he going to extract from me?

My eyes rested on Tee, who was chatting to Justice about Faerie. I'd forgotten how many times we used to sneak in there as young adults. It had been forbidden then, and the moment anyone said the word "forbidden," Tee was all over it. She'd hated rules. Still did, I could tell, even though she was much better at faking it now.

"Are you ready to go?" I hated to interrupt her; I loved watching her face so animated as she laughed and talked, but we were on limited time.

She smiled at me, and just like the last time she did, it felt like something slammed into my chest. "I'm ready." She slid closer to me and I wrapped her up. I had to touch her. It was a need now, and one I expected would only get worse as time went on.

Jacob and Justice studiously ignored each other as they moved closer. The silent feud they had going on was probably going to explode in their faces sometime soon, but for now they were perfecting the ignoring each other thing.

Opening the step-through, I quickly ushered the others in before I followed. On the other side was an empty white room. "Take your shoes off," I warned before I quickly shed my boots, dropping them against the wall in what was clearly a designated shoe section.

"What is this room?" Tee asked, looking around. Her eyes were wide as she took in the starkness.

I shrugged. "Brady is a bit of a germaphobe, mainly with shoes. He doesn't trust where you've walked. Or that's at least what he says. Try not to touch anything, and we'll be all good."

She attempted to cut off her grin, but I saw it. Tee would probably be internally laughing the entire time she was around the fey, but I understood that his obsession was out of his control, and I accepted him for what he was: a loyal-to-the-death friend that I could always rely on. If having that sort of friendship meant putting up with some quirks, I would gladly accept that.

"Brady," I called, and a door appeared in the previously doorless room.

I went through first, because it was in my nature to want to assess danger before my friends or family faced it. That urge was especially strong now that I had a true mate.

Brady waited on the other side, shifting from foot to foot, his hands wringing in front of him. His smile was strong and genuine though. "Louis!" he said with force, rushing forward to me. He stopped himself just before touching me though, because he didn't like to touch. "I'm so happy to see you."

His white-blond hair was shaved very close to his head, because he felt the cleanest that way, and he wore loose-fitting white cotton pants with a matching shirt. His startling blue eyes were fixed on mine, and he looked happier than the last time I saw him.

"Brady, I'm so grateful that you allowed me to open a

step-through here. The president probably wouldn't appreciate me opening one into the White House."

His laugh was nervous, and his words were fast and light when he spoke. "Oh no. No way at all. He would be very angry. I have heard from the interns there that he is in a frenzy learning of supes and everything we entail. This is an important meeting, Louis. So much rests on it."

I nodded, worry pressing on me. I hated walking into situations where I had no clue what was going to happen. Usually I was prepared for anything, but even my guild contacts had no idea what the president wanted with this meeting. He had not spoken to anyone of his intentions.

"Would you like some refreshments while you wait?" Brady asked, looking between the four of us. He offered out of politeness, but I knew he was stressed that one of us would actually take him up on it.

"No, we're good," I answered before anyone else could. I paused then as I received a time for our meeting. When the voice faded from my mind, I straightened. "Looks like he wants us there straight away, so we'll head out now, Brady. It's a twenty-minute walk to the White House."

Brady clasped his hands together tighter, nodding over and over. "Yes. Yes. No worries."

He led us through a very simple white house. He had only the essentials he needed for survival, and everything was clean enough to eat off. I wasn't sure the last time Brady had left his house, relying solely on guild members to keep him fed. He waved us off at the door, and we stepped out into a small courtyard garden, which faded away the moment we left his property. All of our shoes were sitting nearby on the pavers, and we pulled them on quickly.

"Holy shit," Justice said when she was done, her eyes darting from the gray sidewalk to where the garden had just been but was now not visible at all.

"He's a little paranoid," I said with a chuckle. "But loyal to a fault."

No one said anything more; we all got the loyal thing. Tee pressed into me, and I imagined the freedom just to haul her into my arms and disappear somewhere. To love her like she deserved, to worship her body in the way I dreamed of, to crush our souls tightly together so both of us could feel the full effects of the mate bond.

But unless I fixed this huge fucking problem, there would be nothing like that in our future. I would be putting out fires and fighting the human government for years.

"So the meeting is when exactly? Who is feeding you information?" Jacob wanted to know.

I met his startling fey eyes. They had changed slightly now that he was dragon as well as fey, but there was no denying the unusual color. "I've left open some lines of communication between myself and one of the guilds. He is relaying information to me from the president. Also, the elders are coordinating it all."

Jacob shook his head. "The power you wield is stupid. I hope you know that."

I shrugged but didn't argue. It was stupid, but I was used to it now. As long as I never went dark again, the world should be fine.

The streets grew more crowded the closer we got, and when we saw a small vendor on the side of the road selling hot dogs and a few other items, all of us stopped and grabbed some food. It had been a long time between meals, and we had no idea how long this meeting was going to last.

Justice groaned. "It's been forever since I ate human food like this. You know, the nasty kind that will probably give you heart disease or cancer." Another huge bite followed by another groan. "I've missed it," she finished, mumbling around her mouthful.

Jacob raised an eyebrow, watching her with fascination. "You don't have to worry about heart disease or cancer, and in my opinion, you're enjoying that far too much to give up junk food now."

She tried to glare, but her enjoyment was too great, so she settled for flipping him off.

Just when we finished our food, I got another message. It was time to go. "We're ready," I told them.

We were about to step into a world I was not sure of, so I tucked my mate under my arm, keeping her close to me. "I think it's best if we all keep our mouths shut," Jacob said, when we neared the guarded gates. "Let Louis do the talking."

Justice glared, and I hid my smile. It had been pretty clear who he was talking about, and she would no doubt get revenge on him sooner or later. When we reached the guards, I explained we had a meeting inside. They asked for our names, and took a long time checking everything before they searched us all thoroughly and allowed us to enter.

"Did he think we were going to sneak in a human weapon?" Justice scoffed under her breath before sneering at Jacob when he mimed a zipped lip at her.

Guards remained with us the entire walk toward the White House, and I wasn't surprised to find more lingering around the edges, including a few snipers on the roof. I sensed the target on my back, but since I could disable everyone there in a fraction of a second without even breaking a sweat, I allowed them to think they had the upper hand.

The aim was to not start a war, no matter how much they pissed me off.

When we were inside, armed guards surrounded us, and they were not even remotely discreet about it. Tee shot me a small smile, and I knew she was thinking the same thing as me. Humans were always waving their guns around trying to figure out whose was bigger. There were better ways to get what you wanted, but clearly the president was going for the intimidation factor.

"Hurry up," one snarled near Tee, and my fingers twitched as I thought briefly of sending him flying across the room. If they kept waving guns in my mate's face, they were soon going to realize how outmanned and outpowered they really were.

Leveling my eyes on the one who was still far too close, I stared him down. It took less than a minute before he backed up, and then I pushed down my darkening energy, continuing to walk forward. The president waited for us in the Oval Office, and there were upwards of fifty armed guards there. I could see by the cold and calculating looks in their eyes that these were highly trained in their field. Navy SEALs. SWAT. Special Forces. You named it and the president had it surrounding him right now.

He looked quite nervous behind his desk, fingers

steepled in front of him. There was no paperwork or anything else close by, just a cleared desk separating us. I waved a hand, and there were a lot of tense jaws as fingers tightened on their guns.

"There is no need for this," I assured him, moving much slower now so as to not startle them again. "We're here to ensure peace remains between our people. Definitely not to start a war."

A tic began in the president's jaw as he opened and closed his mouth a few times. Finally he spoke. "You're the ... magic one?"

John Caine was an older man, nearing his late sixties, but he'd stayed trim and fit, with very few lines around his eyes. The fear he was displaying now though spoke of a weakness in his soul, and that never boded well for the leader of people.

"I am a magic user," I said calmly, leaving my hands where they could see them. I had most of my attention on the man before me; the rest was reserved for Tee. Keeping her safe was my number-one priority. "I'm also the chosen representative for the supernatural people."

He flinched. Minutely, but it was there. He didn't like to hear our race spoken about so casually. "I'm surprised you have so many humans in the room. What if they talk about this?" I asked.

He shook his head. "If any of them mention this day, the penalty is death. And not just death for them, but also their families."

No wonder there were multiple grim faces in here. Tee spoke up, her voice cold as she glared at him. "Because you're weak, and you fear what you don't know, you would threaten innocents?"

He looked taken aback, especially when he stared at her beautiful, flawless face. "I ... I'm the president. I must ensure my safety. My country's safety."

Her glare didn't falter, and he almost shrank back against it. "What are you?" he whispered.

"Sorceress," Tee said with pride. "Magic user, just the same as Louis."

The president's eyes flicked to me for a moment before they went back to Tee. "You're very beautiful," he said slowly, almost mesmerized. "Like an angel, or a fairy. Far more beautiful than a human woman."

A low growl ripped from me, the darkness pushing my possessiveness up another notch. "Why did you call this meeting? My elders said that there were very few humans who noticed the spell that briefly revealed our existence. We have no reason to be here today."

Especially since there were now a ton more humans that knew, and no matter the threats, people always talked.

"I need to gain control of this situation," he muttered, before finally standing. He was half a foot shorter than me, and he didn't like that, but he held his ground. "I cannot have beings that I cannot control running around my country."

I let out a low rumble of air. Exactly what I thought was going to happen. It was about to be a pissing contest. "We have existed side by side with you for centuries," I told him bluntly. "There was never a time humans were here without supernaturals. It started with the ancient Atlanteans, and then it was the fey, when most of us crossed over. You have nothing to fear from us; we aren't about to start controlling humans now."

The president seemed to think on those words, watching me closely. As if he needed the distraction, he turned to Jacob and Justice then. "What are you two?"

Jacob grinned, but it wasn't a nice smile. It was one that promised death if this fucking idiot didn't rein himself in. I wondered what the protocol would be if Jacob did actually rip the president's head off.

"We're fey," he said shortly, smoothing back his blond hair. "Elemental in nature, we can control fire, wind, water, air ... among other things."

Someone close by started murmuring, saying something about movies, but they cut that off as soon as the president glared in their direction. He then faced us again before walking closer, as if to prove his own bravery. He leaned back on the front of his desk, parting his arms. "What would you have me do?" he said softly. "Just allow you all to go back to your lives? To have an entire section of *supernaturals* living in America, not paying taxes, not participating in our country, not ... protecting our country."

And that's when I realized what he wanted. What this entire meeting was about.

The president wanted to build an army. He wanted supernaturals to go to war for him.

Before he could say another word, I released Tee and let my power pour from my hands. It arced between my palms in bolts of lightning. Dozens of guns were suddenly firing at us, but a second burst of power shot a shield around us, blocking any attack. The president remained on the inside of our shield, his face drawn in terror as he looked around, realizing the position he'd put himself in.

My magic continued to shoot back and forth, and I had to admit, a lot of it was for dramatic effect. Because I had a fucking huge point to make.

"We will go to war for no one," I said quietly, stepping closer. He shied back, halfway up his desk now. "If you try to use your influence to make that happen, I will end you where you stand and deal with the consequences of that later."

He choked. "You'll be hunted."

I shrugged. "Right now I'm prepared to negotiate, because I don't want a war. But I have all the power here; you need to remember that."

My energy didn't want to go back inside. Ever since the darkness, it had been so much harder to control, but with a little help from Tee I pushed it down. The four of us were eyeing the president closely; his normal skin color had paled to something almost sickly.

"I want to know everything about your society," he said slowly, as if he was trying to reorganize his thoughts. "I want a direct liaison ... one who can teach me and also ... protect me from attacks. While I figure out how we're going to coexist."

He clearly wanted a supe with him that he could study, to no doubt weed out our weaknesses. He then swung in Justice's direction. "I want her!"

Jacob's growl ripped across the room, and I felt the heat of his fire before it even appeared in his hands. The president was fascinated with that, his eyes locking on the small flames. "I will not negotiate anymore," he said, swallowing hard. "For now, I will keep this above top secret. I will allow you to go back to your way of life, but I expect to be involved in this new world. Which means you need to leave one of your people with me. One you trust. And I choose her."

"Not without me," Jacob said gruffly, but he did extinguish the flames.

The president seemed to consider this for a beat before he nodded. "Yes, okay, I will agree to that. You two will be brought into my Secret Service guard, and you will be with me day and night."

"For how long?" Jacob bit out. "I have another community that I'm a leader in, and I need to be able to check back in on them."

"Same," Justice added.

The president seemed to consider this, and even though I could sense his nerves, he was hiding it better now. "Three months. Then we can meet again. Figure out the future for both of our peoples."

Jacob turned to me, and I could read the worry in his face. He wanted me to say no, but for now I thought it was a good compromise. The president was going to realize quite quickly that he couldn't control us like his humans, and that we were to be feared and respected. It was good for him to find that out now.

"We agree," I said. "For three months, Jacob and Justice will be part of your secret service. But—" I said, when he opened his mouth. "They will be free to leave in reasonably regular intervals. Both of them have lives and responsibilities in our world, and sometimes that will have to take precedence."

His jaw clenched again. "Fine. I agree. Now can you lower the barrier?"

His people had stopped shooting at us some time ago, all of them clearly able to see that he was okay. I dropped my magic and wasn't at all surprised by the hostility that was being directed my way.

"I expect you to report to work this afternoon," the president said. He then turned and jerked his head at one of the men closest to him.

"Marcus will show you the ropes." He waved the man over. "He's a highly skilled soldier, and has saved my life more than once."

Marcus looked like he'd rather be doing anything other than assisting supernaturals, but he was a good soldier and didn't argue with the president. Lowering his gun, he saluted his boss before turning cold gray eyes on Jacob. "Come with me. We need to outfit you in our suits so that you blend in."

Jacob just nodded.

"What the fuck am I? Chopped liver?" Justice asked, hands on her hips. "I'm gonna need a suit too, asshole."

He snapped her a hard look, only backing down when Jacob stepped in front of Justice. Who immediately pushed him out of the way so she could eyeball the human. It was clear that Marcus wasn't a fan of women soldiers, which was probably going to lead to some epic showdowns. Clearly, he'd never met a supernatural woman, because if he had he would not be discounting Justice. Not for a moment.

"We probably have something for you too," he said reluctantly, seeming to want to keep the peace.

The president looked at me then, and he betrayed his nerves by quickly shooting another glance at my hands, like he was waiting for my power to appear again. "I'm hoping we can make this work," he said slowly. "Our peoples coexisting."

I smiled, and I knew it wasn't a nice smile, because he flinched. "Here's something you need to understand, Mr. President. We're not people. We're supernaturals. And we don't need you. We have existed outside of human control and rule for longer than you've been a civilized nation. Keep that in mind the next time you try to negotiate with us."

I dismissed him then, turning to Jacob and Justice. "Report back in relation to your treatment here. I'd hate to think someone was taking it upon themselves to try to break one of us."

I said this loud enough for everyone in the room to hear. Jacob just laughed. "I'm looking forward to their attempts," he said, and I met his grin with one of my own. Yes, he was going to teach them a thing or two. Of that I had no doubt.

## 26

## ELIZABETH TERESA MONTGOMERY II

*O*utside of my small community in Alaska, I hadn't had much experience with humans. Not in the last twenty years anyway. The human president was no doubt a scary man in his world, but compared to most of the supes I'd met he seemed weak and ... small. I could have taken him down so easily, and he was all bluster until Louis released just a tiny fraction of his power.

"I don't like leaving them there," I said as we left the building. We were trailed by dozens of armed guards, and I felt the energy of many more on the buildings around us. "I'm not sure I trust that man, even if we do have him scared right now."

Louis kept me close to his side, and while his face was the picture of relaxed calm, there was turmoil inside of him. Our bond was thrumming with his energy, and the darkness was pushing forward.

"We have no choice right now. I can't go to war with the humans, not without speaking to the rest of the elders and council leaders. The situation has changed. My time-line shift did delay this knowledge to the wider popula-tion, but apparently fate has decided this is going to happen. One way or another."

"Maybe we figure out the best way to reveal ourselves? A way that will make the humans less fearful of us."

He shot me a slow smile. "Like we turn into super-heroes and start trying to save them?"

I snorted. "Imagine Braxton in tights and a cape."

Louis laughed out loud. "He would shift into a dragon and chargrill anyone who suggested that."

We were outside of the imposing fences now, and I couldn't help but turn back and stare into the huge white building. The armed forces were still lined up across the grass, watching us, waiting for us to completely leave. They were drawing a lot of attention from the humans walking past and gawking through the fence. We were getting just as many looks, and I knew they were wondering who the hell we were to require such a strong armed presence.

Louis and I walked away casually, not doing anything to draw more attention to ourselves, and thankfully by the time we got a few blocks away no one was looking at us. Well, women were looking at Louis, but that was in the normal "there's a six and a half foot supermodel dude with purple eyes" way, not in the "they're terrorists" way.

Louis made sure that we were completely out of sight before he opened the step-through back to Stratford. When we arrived, we went straight to the Compasses' place. "Are they going to be angry?" I asked, already thinking of them as friends and family.

Louis' jaw tightened. "They won't be angry, but they don't like members of their family to be missing. They'll want Jacob and Justice back."

When we got there, the others were waiting, and I knew Louis had called them. "Where's Jake and Justice?" Jessa demanded as soon as we walked into their main living area. "Your message was confusing."

Louis told them everything, including the thinly veiled threats to use and abuse supernaturals to win human wars. I could feel the growing unease amongst them all.

"Are there any weapons they have that would work against us?" Maximus asked, his voice rumbling as his fangs flashed. He was not a happy vampire right now. "I mean, just using my compulsion alone, I could control humans with ease. I've done it before. We can't really have anything to fear from them, right?"

"They outnumber us," Mischa said softly, hugging her child close to her chest. Lily was sound asleep, her perfect little face relaxed, completely oblivious to the worry in the room. "They outnumber us by a lot. Could sheer strength in numbers best us?"

Louis laughed, and suddenly he had everyone's attention again. His power trickled around in a swirl of icy energy, and on instinct, I wrapped my hand around his, pulling him back from the darkness. "Humans cannot best us, not even if they had ten billion more people than us. I could kill a million of them without even breaking a sweat. Elizabeth could probably kill two million. Whatever army they bring at us, they cannot win, but..." The silence was heavy. "We don't want it to come to that. We don't want to fight or enslave or control the humans. But the way they fear, and the way that fear makes them do stupid things ... I'm mildly concerned about the future."

Grace seemed contemplative, her gentle features relaxed. "This might be a good thing. The president will see firsthand through Jake and Justice that we are much stronger than them and that we can't be controlled."

"We should also visit them. A lot," Jessa added, looking unhappy. "I don't like the thought of not seeing them for three months."

I agreed with her. "He will allow them to return home at different times as well," I reiterated, not sure if they missed that part in the discussion before.

Some of the anger and tension faded from the group then, and they all relaxed. Braxton held the only awake child, Jackson, who was playing with a small dragon toy, waving it around.

"So ... what do we do now?" Tyson asked, pulling Grace to him. I noticed that all of the Compasses kept their mates close to them, especially during stressful times. We were the calm to these powerful men.

Louis shot me a slow grin, and my blood started to heat. I smiled back. "Now we go about our normal lives. We wait and see. I'll organize another meeting with all council members and elders. They need to be informed about what has happened, and then ... we wait for the next demand."

Because we all knew there would be another one. The president would not give up his end goal so easily. Only time would tell.

~

LOUIS WRAPPED his hands over my eyes, and I laughed. It was such a happy, carefree sound, and part of me couldn't believe my contentment.

"Where are you taking me?" I asked, not really caring where it was as long as we were together.

His hands blocked my eyes as he guided me forward. "You'll see," he murmured close to my ear, his lips grazing my neck and sending goose bumps across my skin.

I was desperate for some alone time, and I was really hoping this place included a bed and ... a bed, pretty much.

The cold danced across my skin a moment later, and I smelled the familiar scent of my home. Louis lifted his hands, and I let out a happy sigh. "I'm surprised," I said. "I didn't think you'd bring me back here."

We were standing in front of my log cabin, and it looked absolutely beautiful in the low light. Pretty soon the sun would set and not rise again for months, and I loved the cozy half light of Alaska in winter.

"This already feels like home to me," he said softly. "I spent a lot of years coming up here, watching you live your life. Missing you."

My throat got tight and I couldn't speak, but Louis understood, pulling me back into him and wrapping his arms around me. We stood like that for a few moments, until I couldn't stand it any longer. I spun in his arms and threw myself at him. Our lips met, both of us desperate for the same thing. We might be on the brink of a war, but that didn't mean we stopped living. No one knew how many days they had left on this world, and we had to live for each moment.

I didn't even realize Louis had lifted me until we were

inside, my alarms all disabled by the powerful mage. I let out a low cry when he kissed down my neck and across the top of my breasts.

"I'm going to need you to get more naked," I said breathlessly, sending my magic out to strip us both. Louis groaned into my skin, and I could feel the hard length of him pressed against my stomach. We dropped down together onto my bed, and he didn't let me go for a moment. His fingers traced along my body and slid across my center. As soon as he hit that spot, pleasure spiraled inside of me.

I was ready. So ready.

Louis lifted himself above me, our eyes meeting as emotions crashed inside. There was so much in that look. So much—

"Love," he said, reading my mind. "I love you, Tee. You're my world, and I will make sure you're always safe."

As he slid inside of me, a low sob choked out of me, and I reached up and threaded my fingers through his hair. "I love you too, Louis. No matter what life throws our way, we will always be together."

Further conversation was cut off as he loved me in ways I'd never felt before. Every touch carved his name further into my soul. The last time we'd been together, it had been fast and passionate and filled with a desperate need to sate our lust. This time ... this was about love that went deeper than tragedy. Deeper than the lost years between us.

This was our second chance love.

Forever love.

## 27

## STAY UPDATED

*F*or a free copy of The Siren's Alpha and to be signed up for exclusive content from my newsletter (including another serial free story), click here: https://dl.bookfunnel.com/7godch557k

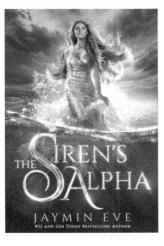

Blurb: Every year Lettie makes the trip back to Hotel Paranormal - a hotel which is used exclusively by a multitude of supernatural beings. This is her one chance to release her glamour and spend time with her siren sisters.

This year the wolves are there too. Including Axel, an alpha wolf, who leads his people with a iron fist and a darkly captivating presence.

The last time they were at the hotel, Lettie and Axel

spent one night together, and this year he plans on tracking her down again -the siren who sung a song around his soul.

Only sirens don't settle and alphas don't mate outside their pack. There is no white picket fence in their future.

It's a battle of the wills, with explosive chemistry, and two alpha supernaturals who will learn that above all else, love is worth fighting for.

# ACKNOWLEDGMENTS

Wow! I mean, really, wow. I almost can't believe I finally wrote Louis's story. This has been a long time coming in the Supernatural Prison world, but I just couldn't get his story out the way I wanted to. Until now.

Louis and Tee, their story is decades in the making, and it was always hard for me to convey the emotions and history between them. Honestly, their love gave me both tears and goosebumps.

I'm so grateful to all of the readers that have stuck with me since 2013 on this series. Following the lives of my favourite supes. It isn't over now either, we still have Jacob's story, and my new Supernatural Academy series is set in the same world (not with the same people etc, but same world building) so there is no need to say goodbye just yet.

Thank you to my lovely editors and cover artist, for shining my words, and putting the most beautiful bow on the package. Tamara, Lee, and Liv ... you absolutely rock!

Thanks to my review team, for your love and enthusiasm. You're part of my pack and I'm keeping you. No take backs.

Thanks to Heather for tirelessly working to promote and support and inspire me. Your friendship means everything.

Thanks to my Nerd Herd for being the most awesome group of humans on the planet. Legit. It's science.

XXOO

# ABOUT THE AUTHOR

Jaymin Eve is the Wall Street Journal and USA Today Bestselling author of paranormal romance, urban fantasy, and sci-fi novels filled with epic love stories, great adventure, and plenty of laughs. She lives in Australia with her husband, two beautiful daughters, and a couple of crazy pets.

https://www.amazon.com/Jaymin-Eve/e/B00E1URI2I

# ALSO BY JAYMIN EVE

**Supernatural Academy (Urban Fantasy/PNR)**

*Year One* (May 2019)

**Dark Elite Series (Dark contemporary high school romance)**

*Book One:* Broken Wings (March 2019)

*Book Two:* Broken Trust (June 2019)

**Secret Keepers Series (Complete PNR/Urban Fantasy)**

*Book One:* House of Darken

*Book Two:* House of Imperial

*Book Three:* House of Leights

*Book Four:* House of Royale

**Storm Princess Saga (Complete High Fantasy)**

*Book One:* The Princess Must Die

*Book Two:* The Princess Must Strike

*Book Three:* The Princess Must Reign

**Curse of the Gods Series (Complete Reverse Harem Fantasy)**

*Book One:* Trickery

*Book Two:* Persuasion

*Book Three:* Seduction

*Book Four:* Strength

*Novella:* Neutral

*Book Five:* Pain

## NYC Mecca Series (Complete - UF series)

*Book One*: Queen Heir

*Book Two*: Queen Alpha

*Book Three*: Queen Fae

*Book Four:* Queen Mecca

## A Walker Saga (Complete - YA Fantasy)

*Book One*: First World

*Book Two*: Spurn

*Book Three*: Crais

*Book Four*: Regali

*Book Five*: Nephilius

*Book Six*: Dronish

*Book Seven*: Earth

## Supernatural Prison Trilogy (Complete - UF series)

*Book One*: Dragon Marked

*Book Two*: Dragon Mystics

*Book Three*: Dragon Mated

*Book Four:* Broken Compass

*Book Five:* Magical Compass

*Book Six:* Louis

**Hive Trilogy (Complete UF/PNR series)**

*Book One*: Ash

*Book Two*: Anarchy

*Book Three*: Annihilate

**Sinclair Stories (Standalone Contemporary Romance)**

Songbird